Sloane Wentworth's deathbed promise to her husband leads her straight to her old flame, Seth, in Truro, Cape Cod. She soon discovers that he's neither friend nor frenemy, but he is trouble, especially when her heart gets involved.

To complicate matters, she still doesn't know why her late husband sent her on this quest, and Seth isn't telling.

Cape Cod's trade winds could blow in the answers, but what happens when she discovers those answers can change her future?

This book is a work of fiction. Names, characters, places, and incidents either are products of the author's imagination or are used fictitiously. Any resemblance to actual events or locales or persons, living or dead, is entirely coincidental.

Cape Cod Connection
Copyright © 2024 Kathy Kalmar
ISBN: 978-1-4874-3911-8
Cover art by Martine Jardin

Published by eXtasy Books Inc

Look for us online at:
www.eXtasybooks.com

CAPE COD CONNECTION
CAPE COD 2

BY

KATHY KALMAR

DEDICATION

To Larry, who gave me my very own second chance to love, more happiness than I could have believed possible, and healed three broken hearts in the process. I swear I can't love you any more than I already do and the next day proves me wrong. It takes a special man to mend hearts he didn't break and children he didn't make. You do that, my love.

In Memoriam
With love
To my forever friend, Linda Wilson, whose skills, talents, and belief in me and my work led to this publication and every book I write. Ours is a relationship forged in the fires of pain, loss, love, and laughter. Living without you is very difficult. You'd love this one!
To Ron Wilson, my best bud, whose deep and abiding friendship led me to Cape Cod.

Acknowledgment

For Carolyn Gilbreath, her counsel and encouragement made this a better book. She is my Best Friend Forever. And with great gratitude, I acknowledge Tina Haveman for her great vision and company, Jay Austin, extraordinary Editor in Chief; Debbie Nygaard, editor, and wise counsel; Martine Jardin, artist; Bri Vries, assistant to the Editor in Chief, The Greater Detroit Romance Writers; Ron and Ginger Wilson who took us all over Cape Cod and introduced us to our special place; Jane Campo, for telling me to keep Cape Cod in the title and you, my readers.
Lastly, Doug Marple, the webmaster, who keeps the social media site wheels turning. I'm grateful to you all.

PART III
DECISIONS

CHAPTER ONE: SHOULD I STAY OR SHOULD I GO

"Apparently, we need to talk," Sloane grumbled at Seth as they walked back to the Paint by Number minivan, the vehicle they had been using all day. *We just had the most terrific day, and hey, I want to savor the afterglow. I can do without the drama.*

Seth stopped cold, shifting the lawn chairs he held as he fumbled with the cooler. "Right here? Right now?"

Before she could answer, her son tugged on her shirt.

"Moooom," Joel whined. "I've got dream crumbs in my eyes, and I wanna go home."

Sloane looked at her sleepy son, who was indeed rubbing his eyelids. She slipped an arm around his shoulders, acknowledging his plea.

She looked back at Seth. "I guess not right this moment. But soon." Something was going on, and she needed to know what.

She had complied with her deathbed promise to Whitt, her late spouse, and had come to Cape Cod and found the mystery man, Joe—who happened to be her ex-flame Seth. Yet she still had no answers as to why it had been so important to Whitt.

Monalisa had laid the law down, ordering Seth to *Tell her or I will*, making it clear that Seth had something to tell her.

What the hell does he have to tell me? I wish he'd just spit it out. I don't have time for this crap.

As the sun lowered in the sky, Seth began loading the

1

minivan, making short work of their beach paraphernalia. "Gotta get the Paint by Number mobile squared away. Why don't you ride with Aunt Monalisa and the kids, and I'll catch ya later? Then we'll have that talk, I promise."

Sloane nodded and rounded up her son and Seth's niece, Janie. After a very productive day, they headed back to the Inn. Everyone looked exhausted. Sloane rode home in comfortable silence with the kids and Monalisa. Seth led the way driving the Paint by Number bus.

Over the next few days, Seth got pulled away in one direction or another, and Sloane stayed as busy as she could. She had kids and a dog to care for since Janie and Whaley seemed glued to Joel during the day, plus the sketches and paintings she was working on.

Seth had both Wing It and Bradford Sail Inn to operate, flights and tours, booth and bookwork, and Janie and Whaley when nighttime fell.

Sloane—not by design and not in avoidance—became that ship that passed in the night.

The still unanswered questions that Monalisa had posed bothered her, but then, so did Whitt's death, its aftermath, Joel's selective mutism, and her future. Her two-week stay at the Inn was nearly at an end, and she had to decide whether to extend her trip or go home to face the legal music still haunting her.

She'd received several cryptic texts from her lawyer and answered him as best she could. However, she and Seth had yet to talk about the mission Whitt's deathbed promise set her on. She was clueless as to what her next steps should be.

She was falling in love with Cape Cod. *I could spend a lifetime here.* And strangely, she thought she might also be falling for Seth.

Sloane loved the suspension of time she experienced on the

beaches of Cape Cod and was loath to leave. The peace she found in the sand and sea could not be duplicated at home. Sure, there was Lake St. Clair and breezes, gulls, geese, and ducks, but there was no long sustained suspension of time. No recuperation. No restoration. No warm, friendly people. Nowhere to heal. The real world was just a few hundred yards from any moment of peace one could find.

In Cape Cod, Sloane could feel she was undergoing a sea change. Her entire perspective was changing as the sea helped her heal from the press of the media and the press and Whitt's death. She couldn't do that on the shores of a lake bounded by land, city, and suburb. Yet she felt torn between the tug of home and the lure of the freedom she experienced in Cape Cod.

Stay or go? She needed some sea magic, sea murmurs, something the sea could toss in her direction that would tell her what to do.

Sloane had also fallen in love with her morning routine at the Bradford Sail Inn. Enjoying the outdoor sea breeze in her flannel pajama with a cup of coffee and sketchbook, her fingers flying over her sketches of horseshoe crabs, oyster shells, sea birds, wave swells, beaches . . . all of it anchored her. Dressing later in the day, gradually, not rushed by a clock, schedule, or a job, held appeal.

She loved wearing casual shorts and t-shirts, coverups, and water shoes. She welcomed the banging screen doors, clacking clothespins, and whistling wind in the seagrasses. To be greeted by the dunes that overlooked the cottages, their long green grasses waving, was not something she was ready to give up yet. Leaving now felt just plain wrong.

Sloane's paintings were due to arrive soon, according to her best bud Addie's text. She had to figure out what to do with them. *Will Monalisa like them? Will another gallery show a few? Can I ply them at Seth's Wing It booth? Display some at local restaurants? So much to think about and . . .*

Seth. What about my growing fascination with him? The fire between us? The race of hot blood through my veins whenever I see him? My heart pounding like it'll burst right out of me? My breath catching whenever he shows up? What about all that?

She couldn't answer all the questions zipping through her mind, so she concentrated on her art instead. Sloane decided to tackle painting the light bouncing off the waves if she couldn't have her way with Seth. Her very *hot* way.

Painting sea light proved difficult to do. Capturing the play of sunrays on the waves, the sea sparkling like diamonds or winking like stars at night presented a challenge. She struggled to render all that.

Sloane couldn't paint the cries, honks, caws, and quacks of the wildlife she heard, but she could paint the waterfowl that made them. At that moment, her skin didn't feel the surge of the sea rushing in, pushing against her, but her paintbrush caught its energy, and the strokes and colors she used did their job.

I have to get all this down. Capture the elusive flashes of light just right. The breeze and the colors teased her. She made them hers, no longer worried if she could paint the splendors of the sea. She was doing it. It was obvious even to her own critical eyes.

Sloane looked up sometime later to see she wasn't the only one to have a routine. Joel and Janie had a rhythm of their own dictated by the tide, wind, and weather. On this balmy day with a pleasant sea breeze, the kids were flying kites with Seth as she painted. Sometimes the children kept busy playing badminton or volleyball, but most days, they busied themselves looking for shipwrecks and buried treasure. Their life on Cape Cod had its own rhythm and flow that only they knew.

She often noticed that Seth didn't rush the children when they stopped to tie a shoelace or when he had to untangle kite strings and relaunch them. He would occasionally pause to ruffle Whaley's fur and accept a slobbery kiss from said mutt. She pictured in her mind's eye a few times when Seth and the kids were flying kites on the Commons' green grass. He always took the time to help both children adjust positions, tails, and angles created by obstacles, changing winds, and other kids' kites. He'd stop in his tracks to make tails longer or shorter.

Sloane recalled Seth's reaction one time Janie was having a rough day.

"Help! Uncle Joe, I need help," Janie complained, looking over her shoulder as she ran to keep her kite afloat, not seeing the driftwood log ahead. "Uncle Joooe, help me. You're always working with Joel. Hurry."

Janie tripped over the log, and both she and the kite hit the ground. She burst into loud tears. Seth was next to her in a flash, kissing her knee with sympathy and tenderness. When he talked to — not at — her, Sloane didn't hear a reprimand of any kind. He set Janie straight and got her kite up and flying again, and all was right in the world. No fuss. No muss.

Sloane chuckled at the memory. *No doubt if it had been me, I might have told Janie something like . . .* Be nice, *or* Wait your turn. *Hmm. A part of me fears I might have snapped and said,* Shake it off.

She admired how Seth interacted with the kids. He was patient, kind, and tolerant, and Joel seemed to thrive under his tutelage. To his credit, Joel hadn't done or said anything to make matters worse. Maybe the whole thing went over Joel's head. *Or maybe your kid is a good egg.* She smiled at the thought. The color was returning to Joel's cheeks, freckles blossomed on his face, and she swore he was growing by the minute right before her eyes. *I don't want to go home now. Leaving might cause a setback for Joel.*

Besides, how can I leave all this?

Saturday arrived, which meant Seth and Monalisa were very busy as guests departed and new ones drove or flew in. Sloane noticed more and more that Monalisa's movements were off kilter. Sometimes she appeared to be catching her balance. *Is it age? A medical issue? Should I say something?*

She shook off her worry as she watched the cleaning crew and maintenance people using check-out time well. They worked from dawn to dusk, maintaining the commons, cleaning the emptied cottages, stripping bedding, and sweeping sand from the linoleum floors. But they did it on Cape Cod time, not city time. They seemed immune to any real-life stress and took the guest turnover in stride. *Maybe the sea winds blow their cares away like the tissues from their cleaning carts.*

For Sloane, the sea winds blew hope and possibility. She inhaled the healing salt-drenched air and accepted the liberty it held. Accepted its abandonment of mundane cares and merciless worries. Felt its freedom. Something within her soul came alive, and she could feel herself healing. And with the healing came the opportunity to desire. She felt as if she had a second chance. To live? To be happy? To love? More than just a chance to recuperate and grow strong. More than a way to stake her claim and create her own brand. More like a promise to become her true self once again. With a man.

She smiled at the sea. Not just any man. One certain man.

Unfortunately, she'd had very little time to talk to Seth lately since she barely saw him. Although Sloane enjoyed her communion with sea and shoreline and watching Joel and Janie, she longed for a chance to have some alone time to simply talk with Seth. Well, and more beach sex like they'd shared the other day.

She recalled his hot lips, the fire in her belly, his firm hips, and his corded muscles bringing her closer to him as she caught each thrust he made until her center spasmed with pleasure. His wet kisses drove her insane with need. She wanted more.

Sloane opened her heart again, accepting the beauty, the calm, the balm this trip promised. Here — if anywhere — she could *almost* believe in happily ever after again. *I want to stay put.*

Sloane's soul had found solace and peace on Bradford Sail Inn's shore. The sea became her church. A place where she found rebirth and the courage to rebound. She looked up to the blue sky and winked. *I know this is You. And this place to me is Cape God from this day forward.*

The weathered boards and shingles throughout Cape Cod were proof of endurance and the certainty that there were things that could withstand nature's fury. If a small piece of land could take the pounding of nature's wrath, then she could surely take a lesson from that. Could persevere and carve out a life for herself and Joel without drowning in Whitt's wake. Could even let herself love again.

CHAPTER TWO: FLY ME TO THE MOON

The children left for Captain Kid's Shipmates Day Camp the following morning, along with several other seafarers in the company's so-called flagship bus. Sloane wiggled her fingers in a *ta-ta* wave as she sent them off. She was happy to see Joel's small face smile again, as if he was looking forward to the adventure. Her phone chirped. She pulled it out of her pocket and saw a text from Seth.

U want to get high? Time 2 fly.

She smiled and replied immediately.

Yes! airplane emoji heart emoji *When?*

Now. Grab your license.

Sloane replied with a thumbs-up emoji.

Seth pulled up in his electric blue *Jeep* with the sunroof open to the warm air and salty breeze. The sun shone overhead on another beyond-beautiful morning. Long streaks of thin clouds crossed the sky like white chalk on a blackboard. When Sloane got into the vehicle, she leaned over and planted a warm, wet kiss on his luscious lips.

"Whoa. Can I have seconds?" Seth stared at her.

She laughed. "Sure."

This time he met her with an open-mouth, heart-stopping kiss that lasted longer than she had intended. Nevertheless, she lost herself in the kiss, combing her fingers through his hair —

An air horn blasted.

Sloane jumped.

Seth jammed on the brakes.

A boisterous bunch of teens in a pickup truck suddenly pulled up next to them.

"Watch where you're going, dude," one kid yelled.

"Kiss her for me, too."

"Get a room."

"Yeah, dude."

Sloane's heart beat fast. She placed her hand over her heart, and once recovered, she giggled. "Keep your eyes on the road, mister."

Seth shook his head. "Said the instigator of said crime — aka major distractor. That was one rude dude. See what I did there?"

Sloane laughed, and Seth glanced at her. "I can see the pleasure in your eyes. I like it." He was also the one responsible for putting it there, so she didn't argue the point.

They were at the small airfield in minutes, and Seth led the way toward the parked planes. "We'll take the Cessna Skyhawk 124 in case you ever need to fly one this size. It seats four. I use it for tours. I'll fly the initial takeoff and landing this time so I can guide you through the winds blowing over the Cape. There's usually some sort of turbulence. The air here can be tricky. And before you correct me, I know you're experienced, but there are some new ropes I need to teach."

"Well," she drawled, "since you put it that way . . ."

Seth grinned. "I'll gladly let you do the preflight checks."

Sloane exited the plane to begin the preflight process — whether she agreed with it or not — and automatically returned to the pilot seat to complete the cockpit checks.

"What? No complaints from the peanut gallery?" he asked. "Where is Miss-I'll-Do-It-Myself, and what have you done with Sloane Somersan?"

Sloane winked. "She grew up. She welcomes this gracious opportunity to fly, skipper."

Seth's face registered surprise. "This is a shock."

"I'd rather it be a turn-on. It is for me."

He winked back, his dark eyes bright in his tanned face. He slanted a smile in her direction. "Same here, but focus. Keep your eyes on the skies—not on *me*, as much as I hate to say that. Safe, not sexy."

"Aye, aye, Capitán. I approve highly of safe sex." She held back a laugh when she noticed Seth struggling to keep his face serious and his gaze steady.

Seth talked her through the tricks of calculating, climbing, and flying in the Cape's windy skies. He threw in pointers as the need arose. Once they were underway, he began the travelogue he used with tourists. "I am your captain, Seth Joseph Bradford, at your service. Today's flight will take us up to a cruising altitude of fifteen hundred feet as we begin our Circle Island Cape Cod Excursion. Our altitude currently is one thousand feet. The air temperature is a balmy eighty-one degrees. You'll note there is no control tower on this field, but I have twenty-plus years of experience behind this wheel. We're leaving Provincetown Municipal Airport at o-nine-hundred, and our return flight will have us landing at approximately eleven hundred . . ."

Sloane wanted to punch him, but this particular flight was new and exciting for her. She had flown over the Great Lakes waters here and there but never over the real open ocean. The winds called for quick calculations as well as skill. She made note of how to deal with them. She didn't punch him, but she did poke his side.

"Usually, after that intro, I start the recording. It's here, see?" He indicated the control switch. "But for today, I'll do the talking in the flesh."

Sloane knew what he meant but decided to tease a little. "Okay. Are you using autopilot or giving me control?"

"Huh?"

"How else are you gonna get naked if you're flying?"

He laughed and adopted a parody of the *Soup Nazi* from the Seinfeld TV show, including the accent. "No free show for you."

Sloane snapped her fingers. "Aww shucks, and I so wanted to see that show. No Mile High Club membership either, then?"

"That, my dear," he said with a leer, "can be arranged." He paused. "Later."

"Party pooper."

He chuckled. "You pick the strangest times and the weirdest places to get laid."

Sloane winked. "But I get credit for knowing what I want and with whom though."

"For sure!"

Seth ran through the standard tour procedures and seemed to be having fun treating her as co-pilot, pilot, and tourist all at the same time. His hot glances indicated he considered her in girlfriend territory, and she liked it. She feared her face would crack because she couldn't stop smiling. It almost hurt. To be soaring in the skies again was pure bliss . . . and the company wasn't bad either.

Seth resumed his tourist spiel. "If you look out the windows, you'll see the Truro Vineyards on your left and the Highland Lighthouse on the right. As part of the Circle Island Tour, we'll be flying over the Outer Cape, Lower Cape, Mid Cape, and Upper Cape and return. Each section's title doesn't exactly conform to geography, but it is what it is. Each is unique." He gave her a wink. "Here's where I plug the business. We have tours for each of the island's sections in addition to the Light House Tour, Town View, Sand Dune Trip, and Beach Bum Tour. Wing It has it all, just like Cape Cod. From time to time along the way, I'll be giving you some fun facts and factoids with a few surprises tossed in for good measure."

She chuckled. "What kind of surprises?"

Seth didn't hesitate. "What do you think of this?" In a heartbeat, he pushed the yoke forward, sending them into a steep dive.

Sloane gripped the grab bar. She gulped, swallowed her stomach, and squealed. "OMG, a thrill ride!"

"Don't try this at home." He chuckled as he regained their altitude and cruising speed. "Need any more thrills?"

Sloane could think of a few — *in bed, a real bed* — but said little. "Any scary facts?"

"I have plenty of shark facts. They are a real and present danger. That's why Bradford Sail Inn has a pool. We're within range of Monomoy Wilderness, and the seals there are what Great White sharks like for dinner. There's more than one reason why the rule is *Never turn your back on the sea.*"

"Why?"

Seth turned deadly serious. "Sharks, jellyfish, rogue waves, getting carried out to sea by fierce riptides." His voice dropped low when he said *riptide*. "It's wild out there. The sea is a fickle and cruel mistress."

Sloane's curiosity must have shone on her face because Seth executed a sharp turn, giving her a magnificent view of land and sea. It was a showstopper, holding her spellbound. Distracting her. Rescuing her. Saving her from the grief that suddenly threatened to break her.

"You take the rudder. I'll tell you where to go, but for now, you are in *control.*"

Sloane swallowed hard, pulled herself together, and focused on flying.

She nodded. *And that's how I like it — being in control. But somehow, I'm losing control of myself. I'm supposed to be a grieving widow, not a wandering widow. Not a merry widow. Stop it.* She gave herself a little shake and maintained her focus. Despite the cobalt sea. Despite the golden beach. Despite the handsome hunk beside her. Doing so was difficult. *What an understatement.*

Again, Seth droned on, sounding like a schoolteacher. "On the way back, we'll fly northwest so you can catch a view of Pilgrim Monument on High Pole Hill, a *must-see* I might add." Seth continued his monologue as they flew.

Good Grief. Focus, girl. Hmm . . . I wonder if we could get in cahoots with Monalisa and let the kids have a sleepover at her place? She felt her face flame. She shifted the controls back to Seth. *Let him worry about flying. I can't focus. Just his voice gets me all hot and bothered.*

As much as she loved to fly, she did enjoy playing the tourist for a while. Thoughts of Seth, lovemaking, her future, and her troubles seemed to fly away while they were soaring over outstanding vistas below. The scrub brush covering the dunes made a vivid contrast to the deep green community commons they passed. The quiet of the sky differed from the slap of the sea, the whisper in the breeze, and the sea songs she was falling in love with. *If I'm not careful, I might fall in love – with Seth.* She drew a deep breath.

"The Cape is checkered with bogs, marshes, kettle ponds, and greenbelts featuring a wide variety of wind-bent pitch pine, white oak, black oak, and most fittingly beech—all of them are native trees."

She chuckled when he said beech, deliberately thinking *bitch, pitch, beach* . . . Anything to free her from thoughts of Whitt's death.

"What's so funny?"

So she told him about her internal rhymes and love of puns and language. But not the part about Whitt. No, she didn't tell him that. Or anything about widows. And she certainly wasn't going to talk or think about anything wandering—especially not the potential of his hands wandering all over her.

She laughed. *If he only knew.* "I do have a lot of fun playing around in my head with limericks, synonyms, acronyms, sounds, and whatnot." She grinned. *I'm also thinking of playing around with you, dear Seth.*

"I bet you do." He looked at her, slanting a small smile. "Want to know what I find fun?"

"What?"

He smiled. "You."

"Cuz I'm so easy to entertain? So easy to get?"

"Au contraire, ma chère. Easy when you're high, not when you're dry."

She laughed, opening her heart again. She accepted the beauty, the calm, the balm this trip promised. Here—if anywhere—she could *almost* believe in happily ever after . . . almost. *I want to stay on Cape Cod. I don't wanna go home.*

Seth winked. "I'm not so sure about that. Remember that party of the century? Get you high on anything and your *go-to—*"

She slapped her hand over his mouth. "Do not go there. So embarrassing."

Seth chuckled and changed the topic, pointing out the names of several beaches they flew over. "Here's Head of the Meadow Beach. We're heading toward Ballston Beach, Nauset Beach, and Coast Guard Beach. As promised, here's a fun fact for you. The Wampanoag are part of the Native American Nation that settled in the Cape. "Did you wonder why the Wampanoag call themselves People of First Light? They settled here in the east near the sea and were the first people to see the sunrise."

"As Joel would say, *sick*." She laughed. "Professor Seth, pray, tell me more."

"At the risk of being a bore, just keep listening. Hm, you're rubbing off on me. This rhyming thing you got going is kind of fun. There's a tour for the Wampanoag—"

"Is there an App for that? "

A shadow crossed his face, but it was gone fast. "No, not yet, but we do have a Native American Tour. It's woefully underdeveloped, but I'm working on it. Mallory was developing both, but since her run-in with an explosive device, she's, let's just say, not up to it."

Sloane frowned. "I smell a story here."

The day was bright and crystal clear, with few clouds and moderate winds. The scenery was gorgeous . . . postcard-worthy.

Seth squirmed in his seat. "Interesting choice of words. Mallory's a photojournalist slash pseudo-war correspondent, but her story is for later. Let's just get through my tour talk and save the rest for a better time. There are happier things to talk about."

About thirty minutes later, they were flying over the Sagamore Bridge and the Bourne Bridge. He changed the subject to the history of the two bridges crossing the Cape Cod Canal, which she already knew was man-made.

Her mind whirled. *We're developing a long list of things to talk about later. Whitt, my mystery trip to Cape Cod, Janie, and now Mallory. What's up with that? I have more questions than I had when I first got here.*

"We're halfway now," Seth announced. " After this leg, I'm going to make a beeline for the airport. We'll be there within the hour. We'll get the kids and remind them they have a date with the clams."

"Clams? What do you mean?"

"I promised your son I'd share what Whitt and I did as kids. One thing we did quite a lot was clamming. I promised Joel a clambake for dinner and that we would go on a clam hunt. I'm hoping doing what his dad used to do and going where Whitt did will help him heal and maybe give him a way to cope."

"Impressive," was all Sloane said. In her heart, she felt gratitude and affection . . . and something more she didn't want to label.

As Seth landed the plane, he mentioned that she might like to take some of the other tours while the children were at

Captain Kids.

"That'd be great. Especially if you have some early morning ones scheduled. That way I can sketch and paint in the afternoons undisturbed." She laughed. "If you don't count the noisy sea birds, sea songs, and beach grass lyrics."

He cocked an eye at her. "Are you sure you don't write, too? You sound like a poet."

She laughed. "The sea songs and sea magic are everywhere here."

"Do you want to go clamming with us later at low tide?"

"Sure, since I've never done it, I'm up for trying."

"Change out of those duds and wear something you don't much care about. Mal has some old boots and whatnot that may fit. You'd swim in my boots." Seth eyed her from head to toe.

Did his gaze linger on my boobs? He sure isn't the type to simply appreciate my cute sailor wear with its white slacks and blue and white boatman blouse.

She raised her hands in a salute. "Aye, aye mate."

"I thought I was your captain." He smiled as he opened the car door for her. The sea breeze ruffled his hair as the sun illuminated a lot to like about *his* physique.

Heat rose in her cheeks to the point she could probably toast marshmallows on them. She was sure they were bright red. "Not on land. Here, you're a mate."

The light sparkling in his eyes enhanced his smile. "Sounds sexy to me."

When he turned to walk around the car, she fanned her face. "*Shipmate*, sir," she said when he sat in the driver's seat. "Air and land. Equal opportunity, if you please."

He winked. "Alrighty then. I'll get the kids outfitted and meet you at your cottage."

"What do I need to bring?"

He grinned. "Sunscreen."

This time her *entire* body blushed. Her whole frickin' body.

If it were possible, she'd bet the roots of her hair were at least copper-tinted. She could not wait to get her clothes off to cool down. *Maybe feel his cool hands on my hot skin. Wonder how I can make that happen?*

CHAPTER THREE: COME FLY WITH ME

Fortunately, Sloane had the clothes she wore when she painted her masterpieces. All she needed was Mal's boots. The old screen door banged when Joel and Janie—wearing pirate eyepatches and kerchiefs—rushed in and greeted her with a chorus of *arrghs* and renditions of sea shanties, sea work songs, and chants. She laughed when they started singing *99 Bottles of Beer* but was thankful when they only sang a couple of choruses. Their other sea ditties were intermingled with cries of *Ahoy there, matey*, making her smile. Moments later she heard what sounded like shovels and Lord only knew what all clattering outside.

Seth—wearing a sleeveless t-shirt, fisherman's cap, and waders—called to the children. "All mates to shore. To the port side now. Tasks galore for ye if ye want yer dinner this eve ... arrgh."

The kids ran outside, laughing and whooping.

He gave them a once-over and nodded. "Lady Jane, ye oversee the hand shovels. Joel, ye take the rakes." He handed said items to them.

"Aye aye, Cap'n," Joel affirmed with a salute.

Seth tossed Mallory's boots to her. She turned away from him, raising a foot to the porch stoop and bending to pull the footwear on. Then the realization hit—too late—that her rear end provided a relatively tame but still worthy *free show*. She swore she heard a wolf whistle, but when she glanced at Seth, his face portrayed innocence.

However, he smiled and raised his hat as though venting

heat. "Must be a wolffish or seal whistling."

Sloane smiled, hoping the children weren't catching onto *that*. She needn't have worried. They were already down the boardwalk heading to the shoreline with Whaley — as usual — romping beside them.

Seth hoisted several long baskets and rake thingies into his strong corded arms. Then he grabbed what she presumed must be some sort of catch pail. The contraption was surrounded by a Styrofoam ring with a leash attached to it. She picked up a second catch pail at his feet and followed Seth to the beach.

Sloane brushed her bangs out of her eyes and paused, enjoying the view of the beach, ocean, and eelgrass. "These are different . . . tools."

"They're designed for sea harvesting. The wire basket catches the clams so they can't fall through the tines of the rakes. They're slippery buggers. The catch pails float on the Styrofoam rings. The lead lines keep the catch from floating away from us."

She nodded. "Nifty."

Once the boardwalk ended, Sloane stopped. Seth took the opportunity to rest a minute.

Seth looked at her, sizing up the situation. "Tired?"

"No. Just need to shift things."

He set his equipment down. "How about we share the load? We'll each take a rake, shovel, and catch pail."

She grinned. "Works for me."

The equipment wasn't heavy, but it was bulky, and the sand walk ahead was going to slow them down.

When they reached the shoreline, the kids were eager and as excited as puppies. Their cries carried on the wind. Together they yelled, "Come on, slowpokes."

Seth cleared his throat to begin his how-to-clam spiel. "First thing —"

Janie sighed. "I already know how to do this, Uncle Joe."

Seth threw her *the look*, and she quieted, scowling. That didn't last long, though, when Seth began talking again. "First thing we do is become clam detectives. To do that, we must think like a clam. Where can we be safe? On land? Hmm, where?"

Joel bit his lip, his brow wrinkling as he thought. "In the sea?"

"Kind of, yes. Do you see any swimming around?"

Joel looked and shook his head. "No. But I don't think they swim."

"Right you are, matey. They sink like stones. Would they just lay there in the open waitin' for sea birds?" Seth looked around, gesturing to the squawking birds. Then he pounced on Joel, holding him upside down. "Lookee here," he cried. "See what I found? You look like a tasty dinner."

"Put me down, you old buzzard. I'm not a clam dinner." Once again securely on his feet, Joel's face brightened. "Mud's a good hiding place."

"You got it. So, we gotta hunt the tricky varmints. Mother Nature's friend, the sea, covers them in mud, but they leave clues. We can track those clever clams. We'll discover their hideout. Keep an eye out for mud that looks like a quarter dropped there. That's a true clam digger clue. You can use the hand rakes to uncover the critters. Ready to try it? Eyes down, careful. Oh, and never turn your back on the sea while you clam, fish, or do anything else."

But his warning didn't seem to apply to Whaley. His paws worked fast and furious, digging for clams his way, spraying water, mud, and wet sand on everyone's clothes and faces.

"Whaley!" They all yelled and turned to look at the dog when a rogue wave hit, sending them and their tools into the drink. They scrambled to catch the equipment before it got swept out to sea.

"See what I mean?" Seth sputtered.

As the wave retreated, Sloane sloshed through the ankle-deep mudflat when she spotted a depression in the mud with a spouting stream of seawater shooting in the air. "Hey guys, what's this?"

Seth looked up. "What a find. Use the hand rake and dig. That's a sign the clam's valve—the head—is just under the surface."

Sloane used the long-handled rake. Once she heard it scrape against something that sounded like a rock, she stopped and bent to peer into the mud.

Seth must have heard it, too. "Good detecting. Dig."

Sloane did and raised a muddy clam triumphantly. "Ta-da." Water dripped a dirty trail down her arm. She dabbed at it, making it worse and streaking mud across her top.

"You found one!" Joel's elated yell made her smile.

Squeals from the kids caused Whaley to dance around barking and getting them wet and muddy when he decided to shake himself off. He suddenly plunged in next to Janie, barking and digging frantically. Sure enough, he had spotted a honkin' big intact clam.

Sloane was glad she had Mal's boots as she walked a few steps further in the mud. "Hey, does a donut shape in the mud count?" She raked, heard the hard clang of the rake tines, and hoisted another clam to add to their floating basket.

"If you pound the sand . . ." Seth demonstrated. "Sometimes that encourages the clams to give away their hideaway."

Sloane's feet got stuck in the mud as her ears caught Seth's words. She tried to not giggle like an adolescent. His choice of words, *pound sand*, gave her ideas. *I have something I'd like him to pound.*

Joel screamed with delight in the streaming late afternoon sun when Seth helped him rake away mud and dig up another whopper. "I found one! This is like Easter. Only I'm

21

hunting clams, not eggs." He started digging again. After a bit, he wiped his forehead, leaving a streak of sludge on his face. "This is hard."

And it was. Hard and dirty. Wet and muddy. And more fun than Sloane had had in a long time. The waves washed seaweed onto shore as she battled with the sea to keep her catch. It was of the sea, belonged to the sea, but *she* was in control. If only of this meager catch. *Control over my uncontrollable life may not be possible, but I got this.*

Seth massaged the small of his back as he straightened from his toil in the mud. "The limit's half a bucket per adult. About fifteen. We met the limit. Time to head ashore."

"That's all?" Joel whined.

The breeze was pushing the water inland. The tide was rising once more.

"Yep. We must leave some so they can make babies, or we won't have any in the future.

"Awww, shucks." Joel swiped at the water in disappointment but stopped raking.

As the tide began its slow return, the adults gathered the tools and baskets when Whaley leapt through the incoming waves and knocked the kids down. Sloane looked behind her and shook her head, watching the children splash about. *Maybe the sea will clean them up a tad.*

Not long after, Janie lobbed a fistful of sand and seaweed at Whaley, but it hit Seth, who retaliated with a huge glob of slippery bulbs. The tricky ocean winds shifted, and seaweed soon went flying to unintended targets. A free-for-all broke out, and Whaley's lack of coordination only added to the melee.

Whaley, though, had plenty of reason to stay put. He loved to chase the sea birds. The humongous mutt's romp in the surf splashed her already thoroughly soaked son. Sloane threw her arms up to ward off any further canine brouhaha and safeguard herself from any doggy assault.

But after a few seconds, Joel took advantage of the opportunity to play around in the returning surf — anything to prolong his time in the water. Sloane surrendered to the inevitable since she was also soaked. She dunked herself — just to rinse off — when a big fat wave tossed her around. She finally got her footing and struggled to stand, then sloshed through the shin-high water to exit the ocean. She squinted against the sun's glare and saw Monalisa not too far away.

Smoke was rising from the sand. *What?* Monalisa moved closer to the shoreline, bending over and gathering seaweed. She seemed to be loading herself down with yellow-brown beach weeds.

Monalisa beckoned. "Come help out."

Sloane shielded her eyes. "Okay." She joined Seth close to shore and asked, "What is Monalisa doing?"

Seth raised a hand to the bridge of his brow, shielding his eyes from the sun's glare. "Oh, she's ready for us now."

"Okaaay."

A steady breeze accompanied the remainder of their walk through the returning sea. Plump, now content and quiet, sea birds floated peacefully nearby.

Seth spoke again, answering her question. "From the looks of things, she's corralled Hank and put him to work building a firepit."

"Huh?"

"To bake the clams."

Sloane cast a glance at him as she waded closer. "A bonfire? During the day?"

Seth laughed. "Oh, such a landlubber. We're having a clam*bake*. So, she's coerced Hank — surely you've noticed our right-hand man by now — into making a sand oven. They've lined the pit with rocks. Hank laid a hickory cordwood fire a while ago. Monalisa's preparing to line the bottom with seaweed and layer that with the food and more seaweed."

23

Sloane mused and winked. "Kind of like making lasagna."

He grinned. "Somethin' like that." He took giant steps through the ocean, pulling the sea float pail behind him. It bobbed along like a child's toy boat.

She lengthened her step as the water flowed higher, casting around until she spied Joel. Seeing he was fine, she continued. "How do you know when to add the clams?"

Seth was almost to shore and began pulling their catch basket in. "When the rocks snap and crack or make a pop sound, you add the food."

Sloane caught up to him. "Cool."

The tide crawled higher up the shoreline, leaving traces of shell and seaweed in its wake.

Seth's mellow voice could be heard above the rush of the surf hitting the shore. "Aunt Monalisa needs the clams — here's where we come in. She will make layers of seaweed and —"

"Seafood lasagna." Sloane giggled.

He wagged a finger at her. "Well, if you say so. We add our fresh-from-the-sea clams to the oven first. Then we corral the kids to add another layer of seaweed while Monalisa and I add potatoes, onions, corn on the cob, and if what I suspect is true, lobster. Cover it with a tarp and viola, sixty minutes later, we have a clambake."

Sloane had reached the shore and began to climb the berm between sea and sand. She laid her tools above the drift line. "Awesome." She looked at the angle of the sun. "Does that mean we'll have enough time to clean up from our sea-fight?"

Seth carried their catch to her side. "Yes, ma'am." He nodded to Monalisa and took their catch over to her.

Her attention shifted to the laughter of the children. The tide was rising fast, so she decided to call an immediate halt to their play. She waved to get Joel and Janie's attention. "High tide's coming in. Head for shore. Everybody Out.

Now."

Once Whaley's human pack made a move toward the shore, his antics beckoned the children to land far faster than adult words did. The children followed the mutt like little ducklings.

When Joel and Janie chased Whaley up the berm and across the beach, Sloane released the breath she hadn't realized she was holding. Whaley's beach romp ended with rolling in the sand. The children pounced on him, creating a tangled mess of muddy fur, clothes, and flesh. Sloane shook her head with a resigned sigh, but truth be told, she didn't mind a bit. Joel was having a ball, and so was she.

Janie threw out a challenge. "Hey Joel, can you do this?" She rolled onto her back and started making a sand angel.

Sloane groaned when Joel followed her example. Whaley was already a shaggy, sandy, wet mess. The kids — chests heaving with excitement and exertion — were a messy disaster as well.

Seth just laughed. "Good thing we have outdoor showers and clean clothes."

Whaley apparently knew what was going to happen next. He snagged a beach towel hanging by wooden clothespins on the old-fashioned clothesline stretched between the cottage and post, causing the line to bounce and the clothespins to chatter. He ran to Seth, dropped the towel at Seth's feet, and hung his head until Seth forgave him with a pat on the head. He barked his *sorry*, then ran to the hose lying beside the outside shower and dragged it to Sloane as if doing penance.

Whaley ran back to the showers. The children ran after him. She and Seth ran after all of them. Plenty of outdoor water spouts via hose and showerheads made short work of the muck and mess covering everyone.

When everyone was clean, Whaley did as Whaley always did. He rolled in the seagrass until he was satisfied with his doggy self. Then he settled in for a nap and snored with the best of them.

When Monalisa approached carrying some tools for unearthing their sand-oven dinner, she wobbled a bit off balance. She dropped a shovel. Seth offered Monalisa a steadying hand and led her to the picnic table, where she could supervise and direct the operation.

Monalisa gave him a shaky smile. "This getting old stuff seriously sucks." She raised a hand to her chest and huffed as if winded.

Sloane immediately took control of the shovels while Seth beckoned Hank to help remove the canvas tarp from their clambake. Once the guys set the canvas cover aside, the intoxicating aroma of the meal drew everyone closer. The hickory firewood smoke combined with the scent of potatoes, corn, and clams made her mouth water as she watched Seth carefully rake the seaweed aside. The delicious scent rising from the oven made her stomach growl.

She giggled. "I volunteer to be the taste tester."

"Dig in." Monalisa chuckled.

Sloane looked at her, a bit confused.

"Pardon my pun, but dig in the sand oven, dig out the food, and then . . . well, dig in and eat."

Sloane smiled and nodded, smiling. She helped Seth dig into the pit, raising the steaming fare to the platters waiting on the foldaway tables. The aroma of fresh baked lobster, corn, and clams had the kids running to help.

Carefree, light-hearted banter burst from hungry helpers as everyone worked to get the food onto their plates. Intermingled with a series of delightful cries were plenty of . . . *oops, almost dropped the corn.*

Adults and kids danced little jigs as they juggled hot clams, potatoes, corn, and lobster to plates. A chorus of comments echoed from everyone.

"Whew."

"So good."

"Watch your fingers."

"The foil's hot."

"Be careful."

Sloane chuckled when Seth winced as he peeled the foil from the potatoes. She shook her fingers, blowing on them as she struggled to free a clam from its open shells to plop straight into her mouth. "Oh my God, oh my God, hot, hot," then, "but so good."

Laughter of joy burst out as everyone carried their food from the pit oven to the picnic table. As Joel lifted his leg over the seat, his plates tipped, and he laughed as he rebalanced it.

Cries from Seth and Janie called out, "Don't drop that lobster."

Silence reigned as everyone dug into their food. Murmuring slowly broke the quiet, rising like prayers.

"Yum."

"Outstanding."

"Mm good."

Sloane added her moan of appreciation to the others. Delicate sweet cobs of corn competed with the earthy baked potato, the sour cream cold in comparison. Buttery lobster complimented the sweet onions, and tart cranberry iced tea rivaled cold beers. And the clams. Oh my. How divine. Delicious. This had to be one of the best meals she'd ever had.

She glanced around the table, seeing plenty of fingers in mouths as they licked them. Smiles sprouted. Contented sighs released as bellies filled. And all accompanied by the whispers of the sea winds in the beach grass, the cry of the gulls, the roar of the sea, and the waves pounding into the shore, rocking boats against the dock. It was an altogether wonderful experience. One to remember.

Monalisa rose to begin clearing the table, rocking a bit and gripping the table for balance.

Sloane got up and removed the silverware from her hands. "You've done enough for the day. We're the clean-up crew. You just sit, relax, and enjoy the sunset."

Sloane caught Seth's attention while Monalisa sat back down with a nod and a smile. Sloane stacked the dishes while Seth doused the fading embers and raked the seaweed remnants away. Hank removed the rakes and cleaned the empty clam basket. Whaley, oh so helpfully, pulled the tablecloth off the table and skedaddled with it. Joel ran after him with an armful of beach towels, and Janie lugged the beverage cooler. As everyone worked, the setting sun turned the sky a brilliant pink and purple ombre topped with towering blue-gray darkening clouds.

When everything was complete—

All the eating . . .

All the chit-chat . . .

All the laughter and play . . .

All the cleaning up . . .

Everyone traipsed through the sand back to Seth's cottage. Sloane cleaned each dish and tucked them safely into the cupboard. She then knew she could rest, too, and take in the sense of utter contentment.

Then the pièce de résistance of the evening happened. Seth kissed her—a long, sweet one. She relaxed and let her lips welcome his. She leaned into his firm, sturdy body, yearning for more. More of his touch on her skin, on her belly, on her hips, on her breasts and nipples, on and in her center. She knew then Seth had already somehow managed to sneak some kinda wonderful magic into her heart. She took it all in. Every single sound, sight, smell, taste, and touch. She made it all part of her, letting all of it into her life. Let all of it lodge in her soul.

CHAPTER FOUR: SOMEDAY, LADY, YOU'LL ACCOMPANY ME

The next morning, the fog rolled in. Sloane heard the muted cry and the mournful sound of the foghorn off in the distance. She and Joel walked carefully across the blanketed Commons, fog covering the long beach reeds. As they walked past the docks, they heard groans.

Slone jumped, raising her hands to her heart and emitting a small, embarrassed laugh. "Wooo, creepy, right?"

They heard the old wood of the dock creak again as they crossed its planks. The ropes moaned as they struggled to hold the sea vessels in place.

"Spoooky," she teased.

"Mom. What's that?" Joel asked. "Do you think a Ghost Ship with Long John Silver and his pirates is coming ashore to look for buried treasure? Do you think we stepped on his hiding place?"

The fog in her hair and the cool dew on the grass chilled her. She hugged herself against the damp. She kept her tone low. "Anything's possible. I hear a famous pirate hid out this way."

"Seriously?"

A deep voice pierced the thick clouds covering the marsh on their left. "Aye, that he did, matey. Argh."

Sloane and Joel both jumped as the culprit slowly emerged through the thick layers of fog.

A sudden strong trade wind blew the low-lying clouds

apart, revealing Seth in all his glory. In one swift move, his strong hands reached out and grabbed Joel. "Avast, ye scally-wags, who goes where no man dare?"

"Help, Mom!" Joel doubled over, giggling as Seth lifted him off the ground.

Out of the silent mist came a huge bark as Whaley plowed through them to tug Sloane forward by her shirttail. Seth quickly set Joel down, rocking on his feet and arms flailing as he tried to right himself.

Seth cackled. "Avast, good dog, er, mate, ye found the mu-tineers."

"Says who? What'd I do?" Sloane growled as Whaley pulled her toward the soft glow of a lamppost. "Whaley, down. Stop. Unhand, uh, un-paw me." Sloane emerged through the mist to confront Seth. "I'm innocent. I'm just try-ing to get to my dinghy."

Janie's young female voice joined in the fun. "For your mis-deeds, you must walk the plank."

Seth's deep voice boomed. "That be your mistake, lassie. Ye be trespassers. Tis my dinghy now. I claim it for Captain Sam Bellamy, meanest, baddest, and if I may say, most suc-cessful pirate captain to ever sail the seven seas."

Fog lights pierced the gloom, and the hiss of airbrakes sur-prised pirates and captives alike. They heard the screech of automated vehicle doors opening and a pleasant, quite nor-mal voice calling out.

"Watch your step. Board the bus carefully. We're off to Captain Kids, shipmates. Heck of a morning, eh?"

"Is that you, Jake?" Seth asked. "Aren't you supposed to be at Whale Tales? What are you doing here in a . . . what? A school bus?"

"Stella Kidd couldn't get the ole pirate ship goin' this morning, so I talked to the superintendent, and he let me use the school bus. I'm the driver today. The damp gets Stella's crate every time a cloud creates a mist or spews fog. Ordered a new van, but you know, taking into account the demand and delays, who knows when it'll be ready. This bus is Plan B." Jake motioned to Joel and Janie. "Hop in, shipmates."

The airbrakes released, the gears ground, and the exhaust system belched as the doors shut behind the kids.

Sloane could hear the children chatter as the bus turned onto the road, heading to pirate school.

"You up for a cuppa joe?" Seth looked at her.

She shrugged, "Not if we have to drive anywhere to get it. You think the kids will be safe? In this fog?"

A shadow crossed Seth's features, but it was gone in a second. *What's that all about?* It was too early in her day to look for anything more troubling than the fog, so she made herself stop.

"Aunt Monalisa brewed a pot, and yeah, our pirates will be safe. Jake Issacs used to drive the bus when he coached the football team. He's experienced, he'll keep them safe. They're in good hands."

"Oops, I shoulda known that. Otherwise, you'd never let Janie go with him. Sorry if that offends . . . it's the helicopter mom in me."

Seth opened the screen door to his cottage, led her to the old maple table, and filled two mugs with coffee, offering her one.

Mounted ship lanterns lit the cozy nautical room, creating a soft glow. Knotted gingham yellow curtains didn't block the view. The bay windows normally permitted a great view of the beautiful blue ocean. What she looked at now was pearl gray and not at all glass calm. No, it tossed and churned like a salad of gray and dark green choppy waves. White froth and foam washed up, trimming the shoreline like a ribbon in Janie's hair—bunched here, flat and long there. It created yet another picture she would try to paint.

She stirred three spoonfuls of sugar into her coffee.

Seth chuckled. "Any cream with your sugar?"

"Yes, please."

He winked. "You know you're drinking sugar milk, don'tcha?"

"I prefer to think of it as a coffee latte."

"Whatever. What are your plans for the day? Too foggy to air tour."

Sloane smiled. "Gonna try and catch this mood on canvas. Got some work ahead of me. Mind if I take this to go?"

Seth shook his head. "Fine with me. I'd rather you stay, but as they say, ya gotta strike when the muse does."

She just cocked her head and looked at him. "Says no one ever."

"Don't knock it, lady. G'wan, get outta here. Go paint sumthin.' When the fog clears, I'll be conducting a Lighthouse Tour. You interested?"

"Yes. I love lighthouses. I painted a whole series of them in Michigan. In all seasons."

"Really. Cool. Michigan has the second most lighthouses in the country."

"Who has the most?"

"I'm surprised you don't already know. Cape Cod. Has it—"

"All." She smiled. "I had my collection sent here. Monalisa asked for samples of my work. It should arrive soon, according to the tracking info." She waved ta-ta and left for her art supplies.

The fog seemed to abate a tad, appearing thin and wispy. Once Sloane reached her cottage, she grabbed her sketchpad and charcoal and headed back outside. While she aimed to capture the warring waves that slapped the shore, she looked at her work and gasped. She had sketched a pirate, who winked from the page. He looked suspiciously like Seth. She shrugged. It wasn't half bad. She turned a fresh page to draw the fishnets, anchors, and sailboats moored nearby. They groaned as if protesting their link to the dock and land, straining to be free in the sea.

As the fog began to lighten, sunlight streamed through, turning the masts of the furled sailboats gold and freeing the yellows, reds, and blues of the buoys, too. A plethora of silver-tinged aluminum boats begged for her attention. Laying aside her charcoal, she dashed inside to grab her pastels and watercolors.

After completing a few more drawings, she paused to review what she had created, pleased with her work on two accounts.

First, what she'd drawn was good, really good, recreating the mood perfectly. She had managed to catch the faint sun as it gave birth to a great afternoon with colors ranging from gray to sage sea green to denim ocean blue. She'd captured that momentary sea magic, and it delighted her.

Secondly, there was no trace of a certain sexy pirate anywhere.

Sloane reveled in her communion with sea, ship, and shoreline. Part of her knew there would never be enough paint.

Enough canvas.

Enough sketchpads.

Enough pastels.

Enough watercolor.

Enough ink.

Never enough time to catch everything she saw. Everything she felt. She watched the blue ocean kiss the sandy shore and knew she was home.

Here in Cape Cod.

Home. Four simple letters with a world of meaning. Here, she could be free in a place where no strangers judged. A place that was a haven, an oasis of peace, a pocket of paradise, a promise of dreams becoming reality. She inhaled deeply, loving the brine in the breeze. With each inhale, a new brew of faith and renewed possibilities for herself and Joel found a home. And who knew? Maybe it held a promise of new love that was stewing and very nice.

As the sky cleared, Sloane closed her sketchpad, put away her art materials, and went in search of Seth and the promised Lighthouse Tour.

As pledged, Seth was outside his cottage waiting for her. All six-foot-five inches of him looking hot and handsome. His white teeth and sexy half-smile made a great contrast to his tanned face. *I hope I look as good as he does. He looks like the handsome host of the old Fantasy Island television show. Hmm, maybe Aquaman from the movies?*

"Hello there, hot stuff." Seth greeted. "Look at you, all tan and sexy. Ready?"

Sloane flipped him a perky salute. "Yo ho, off we go, sir." She peered over her large white plastic sunglasses. "What?"

"Nuthin'." He chuckled. "But *Yo ho*?"

"Just practicing my pirate talk. For my next pirate encounter."

He cocked a brow, grinned, and opened the door of the Wing It van. In minutes, they passed along the tall grasses lining the route to the sand-swept airfield.

A middle-aged couple rose from a bench when they saw Seth in his captain hat and official Wing It uniform. He walked forward, extending his arm for a fist bump. He remained cautious even with the virus supposedly in the rearview mirror, and she approved.

"Tim and Elenore Baker? I'm your pilot, Joe Bradford. Our plane is ready for your Lighthouse Tour." He then waved toward her. "My co-pilot, Sloane Wentworth."

I have such a hard time thinking of Seth as Joe. It's like two men

34

in one. Already masked for the flight, she addressed the couple. "I'm smiling at you. You just can't tell with this mask."

Elenore chuckled. "I can tell. Your eyes are smiling."

Tim winked. "I can tell by your sparkly mask. You have a wicked sense of humor."

Seth went about the preflight check as Sloane guided the couple to their seats. Seth started his spiel, giving statistics and weather reports while he taxied to the runway.

Once in the air, Seth talked about the geography, comparing Cape Code to a *bent burly boxer's arm.* Sloane bit her lip to refrain from laughing at his description.

"The first lighthouse we'll see today is coming right up," Seth announced. "It's the Highland Light House, and believe it or not, it once stood directly below us."

They all looked down. The Atlantic stared back at them. There was nothing to see but the ocean.

"Yup. Erosion ate the land away. They had to rebuild it— twice. The original was built back in seventeen-ninety-seven. This one was built about one hundred sixty years ago. They jacked it up, supported it, and put it on rollers, moving it six hundred feet inland in nineteen-ninety-six to where it now stands. Amazing what we can do with old-fashioned ingenuity and a bucketful of luck."

Sloane was impressed by the information and Seth's memory. He sounded like a real honest-to-goodness tour guide speaking with easy confidence, not the firm flight instructor she once knew.

"Remarkable," Elenore said. "Looks like there's a house attached. Can folks tour it?"

"Yes, it's a museum open to tourists. It once housed the lightkeeper and nowadays serves as a gift shop selling things landlubbers like. It operates from mid-May through mid-November and offers—for a nominal fee—a climb up to the beacon. The view is fantastic. Straight across miles and miles of ocean sits Portugal. In fact, many Portuguese came here to work—before the virus, that is. Their influence is everywhere."

Tim spoke up. "That explains the Portuguese bakery we passed this morning. I wondered why a Portuguese shop. Now I get it. They came for work and wanted a taste of home. Can't say I blame them. The sweetbread was to die for."

"The Portuguese cuisine has made a huge impact on the on the Cape. Provincetown has the makings for an exceptional culinary experience—one you won't want to miss." Seth banked to the left, flying overland for a bit. He pointed out the Old Higgins Farm Windmill that stands in Brewster off Old King's Highway. He provided more factoids and then directed their attention to another lighthouse.

"Depending on who you talk to, this lighthouse has had many names. Some have called it Nauset, Nauset Beach Light, Chatham, Twin Lights, Three Sisters, and who knows what else? Its history is complicated but worth repeating—just don't ask me to."

Seth added several fun facts from the local lore, then spoke again after the tourists asked a few questions and finished their *oos* and *ahs*. "I'm not exactly saving the best for last, but to my mind, nothing can top this one."

Sloane looked down and was disappointed. She wasn't sold. "It's not very tall. What's so special about this one? I get why sailors would need a beacon here, but why do you like this lighthouse so much?"

Tim and Elenore craned their necks to look. The blue-gray Atlantic roiled and rushed to shore, slamming into rocks, but the lighthouse was nothing special in her opinion.

"What makes this one so different?" Sloane asked, looking around and shifting her position.

"Well, for starters, Race Point Lighthouse has saved many vessels and many souls. Indeed, it doesn't look like much.

Piddlin' next to others. But in addition to its lifesaving light, it offers three buildings. The Whistle House and the Keepers House, which you can rent and stay overnight, and the light-house, which occasionally offers tours. Solitude and sea splendor . . . a perfect combo. I bet you'd like it."

"Too pricey for moi," she murmured.

"Very few experiences like this anywhere else." Seth continued his spiel. "The interiors of both houses have recently been restored and offer an open layout perfect for allowing the cool ocean air to breeze through the windows. Cross-air ventilation, a light blanket, a lover, what more do you need? The houses offer privacy, perfect for a family vacation getaway or a honeymoon. You can stay for two nights, or a week, more if there's availability — and you have a great income."

"Sounds like we should look into it, Tim." Elenore giggled.

As if he hadn't already said so, he repeated, "You can sleep overnight in the lightkeeper's quarters on Race Point? Not a tent. This is Race Point Lighthouse, and I promise a night here will provide a night to remember."

Sloane grinned. *Of that, I have no doubt Hubba, Hubba.*

Seth continued to discuss the other opportunities abounding in and around Cape Cod. He included a follow-up tour with a land tour offered by Jake Issacs, his tour partner in crime.

Jake was not only in charge of the *Whale Tales Book Shop* in Provincetown but also responsible for land tours Wing It offered.

After plugging several land excursions, Seth returned to the airstrip. When they completed the tour and said their goodbyes to Tim and Elenore, they headed back to the Bradford Sail Inn.

CHAPTER FIVE: RETURN TO SENDER

When Sloane and Seth arrived at the Inn, they were greeted with pandemonium. It looked like every guest and their brothers and sisters were choking every parking spot — available or not. Crosswalks were blocked, and so was the entry to the office. In addition, there seemed to be a parade of delivery vans, trucks, and even a FedEx vehicle.

Sloane gulped, swallowed, and turned to Seth. "What's going on?"

"Shipments must be in." He shrugged, looking as confused as she was.

Workers carrying folding chairs and what looked like a white tent went down the eastern boardwalk to who knew where. To do what? Erect a tent, place chairs, set tables up? Other personnel carried banks of floral arrangements. Boxes filed past held by guests who had apparently been pressed into action while another ran off with *Beach Closed* signs and began setting them up at the intersections leading to the beach.

"There must be something I can do to help. Lead people to the Commons at least?" Sloane spotted Hank escorting a group of delivery men to the maintenance garage and corralling some of the clean-up crew to help.

Seth threw his hands up. "Hell if I know . . . Here, take my phone. Look for Olivia and call her. She'll rally the church ladies' Helping Hands Auxiliary. They organize fast and will know what to do." He appeared frustrated as he looked around. There simply was no place to park so he could get out and take charge. He huffed and whipped the van around to park in the side lot of the Inn next door.

If Sloane wasn't mistaken, several food trucks were moving toward the main house as well. To top it all off, the *Captain Kids* school bus—obviously functioning now—was thrown into the mix. Joel and Janie erupted from it.

Whaley bounded through all the chaos, and the children froze in place, looking entirely overwhelmed. Young gazes darted here and there, clearly not sure what to do. Joel looked terrified.

Sloane carved her way through the crowd to shepherd Joel and Janie through the arched arbor to a safe haven. She snagged Whaley by the collar and dragged him with her, too. She bent to Janie's eye level. "Take Joel to our cottage." Reaching into her purse, she extracted the key and gave it to Janie. "Stay at our place with him. You can watch TV or play in the sand near our cottage, but do not go to the boardwalk. Stay there until one of the adults you know tells you what's up." She bent to give Joel a reassuring hug. "You're okay. There's some yogurt bites to snack on. I'll be with you as soon as we can figure out what's happening."

When she turned back to the crowd, people were congregating everywhere in and around what was beginning to look like a wedding venue. Seth must have come to the same conclusion.

He slapped his forehead. "Holy Shit! The Wilson Wedding party has apparently arrived—early! You'll have to excuse me. I've got to deal with this."

And if everything else going on wasn't enough, Addie was suddenly right *there* in front of her. In Cape Cod . . . maneuvering her way through the madness . . . smack in the middle of the chaos. *Addie*. Her best friend. From Michigan.

Addie burst through the hoard, grabbed Sloane, and started pulling her toward her car, babbling a mile a minute.

"Sorry to show up unannounced, but Adrián contacted me at the last minute about some movers at her gallery to pick up your paintings. I couldn't let some strange movers just take them that way, so I took things into my own hands. I went to the gallery, packed up your paintings, and drove straight here as fast as I could. So here I am."

Sloane's mind whirled, working hard to summarize what was happening. Addie. Was. Here. *And she's holding a ripped package covering a painting — a painting that was at* On the Hill Gallery. Sloane then noticed packaging falling off several other paintings — her paintings no less! Her Lighthouse paintings, to be more precise. They were here. Apparently . . .

Then she caught sight of a delivery guy holding a tall box and searching for someone. She saw Hank point her out, and the young man headed toward her. He would reach her in mere seconds. *No. Just No. This can't be happening. Don't let that be . . .* She glanced around, suddenly confused. "Wh-What? Huh?"

Sloane's mind went fuzzy, her vision cutting in and out. Her heartbeat roared in her ears, and she felt the blood drain from her face. She knew this was gonna be bad, knew she was in trouble.

Then, Monalisa materialized. *How did Monalisa reach me?* The crowd, the hubbub, the chaos, the confusion swirling, and . . . *Monalisa? What? How? Why?*

In moments, Monalisa pushed her and Addie inside the nearest cottage. She grabbed the rope and pulled the clapper of the old sea bell. It rang loud and clear, piercing the noise to summon help. Sloane knew *Emergency Use Only* was written in red over the bell post. *This is an emergency all right.* The delivery kid was closing in. Sloane looked at Addie.

Addie launched into another torrent of words. "This is my fault, Sloane. I got here just as the FedEx truck did. And there's a wedding going on, and there's nowhere to put your paintings. Monalisa took one look at them and went into overdrive. She loves them and has ordered that they be displayed in her gallery! Can you believe it? I had to agree with her. I'm not saying this right. I mean, I'm not telling things in order. You weren't here, and I'm so used to handling things back home that I agreed. I hope you don't mind . . ."

Someone cleared his throat, and Sloane turned to face the delivery guy. He looked uncomfortable but somehow threatening, like he dreaded delivering whatever it was.

His tentative, thin voice bleated, "Excuse me, ma'am. But are you Mrs. Whitman Wentworth?"

Sloane nodded and heard the bell clang again. She swayed, raised a hand to her heart, felt the blood rush from her head . . . *I think I'm fainting.* Blackness fell.

The emergency bell rang clear through the competing melee, the noise, and the chaos. Seth's first reaction was pure, raw panic. Then . . . *Run! What fresh hell? Janie? Monalisa? Joel?* His heart pounding, he ran like he had never run before. He jumped over a short hedge in his way and got to the bell post as fast as he could. He spun, his heart in his throat as he tried to figure out where the latest problem was. And then, clarity rushed in, and he knew, he just knew. *Sloane.* She needed him. He turned to Captain's Cottage and saw Sloane swaying on her feet. He reached her just in time to catch her and break her fall. A thousand questions and all his fears rushed at him, but nothing mattered more than the woman he held.

Seth's voice shook, but his hands were steady as he crooned. "You're all right, baby, you're okay. Everything is fine. I'm here. I'll always be here." He caught Monalisa's attention, and she raced off, returning with the first aid kit.

Monalisa dug inside and extracted a small ampule. She broke the seal and waved it beneath Sloane's nose.

Sloane stirred, opened her eyes, and looked at him, still a bit unfocused. She coughed and sputtered. Her gaze stole to Addie's stricken face and Monalisa's concern.

She looked back at him, confused. "What happened?" She looked around her as if she loathed to sit up and find out, her gaze searching her surroundings. She gasped and clenched his hands.

By the shudder that went through Sloane, Seth knew when her gaze found the object that had caused her condition.

Whitt. His ashes.

The funeral home had FedExed them to Soane at the Bradford Sail Inn. The delivery had caught Seth off guard, too. After all, Whitt had been like a brother to him.

He gave Sloane a half-smile. "You had a huge shock on top of a whole lot of everything in a short time. I got you. You got this." He tightened his hold. "Anyone in your shoes would react the same way. All hell broke loose and hit you like a rogue wave." Seth helped her to her feet.

Sloane raised a hand to her forehead.

Addie made it to her side, holding a shot glass. "Here," she said, "drink this."

Sloane gave a shaky laugh. "Don't mind if I do." Her eyes strayed to the plain white box. "I wasn't expecting it. I should have . . ."

Monalisa patted her shoulder. "We know. We get that. Honey, I'm so sorry . . ." She handed Sloane a bottle of water. "Hydrate. It's good for what ails you."

Sloane's hand was shaky, but she took the bottle and gulped half of it.

Then, like the sun coming through a cloudy day, Sloane's expression seemed to clear. She smiled at Monalisa. "That was a fine kettle of fish. I take it the church ladies have things under control."

Monalisa patted her again and nodded.

Sloane turned to Addie. "Don't fret. Not your fault." Then she zeroed in on him. "We need to talk."

Chapter Six: Troubled Water

Sloane was happy to learn that things seemed to be settling down and under control outside. Monalisa hustled everyone out of the cottage, pulling Addie in one direction while leaving Seth and Sloane to sort things out.

"You two," she said, "go for a walk, and for God's sake, talk. If you don't know where to start, there's always death and summer taxes. In this case, both are relevant." As she began to leave, she added, "Don't worry about the children. They've been bellyachin' for a sleepover to watch *Hook*, so I'll let them and get them off to pirate school tomorrow morning."

Sloane's brow crinkled as she considered the proposal. She didn't really feel up to parenting right then. "Okay. Fine. Thank you."

Seth steered her down the sidewalk away from the wedding pandemonium and led her down the boardwalk that extended beyond the marina, heading toward Provincetown. Benches dotted the expanse, and they found a quiet spot to sit once they were beyond the beachcombers. The silver-tinged waves winked in the sunlight, and the bracing ocean breezes gave her a second wind.

Steadying herself, she took a swig of water, squared her shoulders, and asked, "Why is Monalisa bringing up summer taxes? What does that have to do with all this?"

Seth swallowed. "Uh, you're part owner of the Bradford Sail Inn, and summer taxes are due—"

Sloane jumped up. "What?"

"Didn't Whitt tell you?"

"Apparently not. Seems there's a lot he didn't tell me. Part owner. Of Bradford Sail Inn? Me?" Her voice rose an octave. "I owe taxes? How do I pay for those? How much? This is crazy. Talk to me. My bank accounts are frozen."

Seth's brow wrinkled. "Like, uh, you, uh, usually do. Use your quarterly earnings—"

"What earnings?"

Seth slapped his forehead. "Holy shit. Whitt didn't tell you *anything* about owning half of the Bradford Sail Inn?"

Sloane started to shake. "I don't know what you're talking about. Whitt never said anything about any of this. You better fill me in and fast."

Seth seemed to develop a stutter suddenly. "Er, eh, um, uh ... First, take another swig of the water, and I'll, uh, I'll try to explain."

His consternation warred with concern. That much, at least, was clear. Sloane could hear it in his voice, see it with her eyes.

"I assumed Whitt had said something to you about all this."

"Whitt didn't tell me shit, and I'm sure you know what they say about assumptions. What you assume makes an ass of you and me. So spill, buddy."

Seth gulped. "Okay, okay, uh, I'm not sure where to begin."

Sloane's voice held sarcasm. "At the beginning. Didn't you tell me that the other day? What the hell is going on?"

Seth continued to struggle to explain. "Right, the beginning. You already knew Whitt and I were as close as brothers. Neither of us had a brother, and after Whitt nearly died drowning ..."

"You saved him"—she picked up where Seth left off—"and the two of you became closer than brothers. Yes, yes,

Monalisa told me all about it. What does this have to do with me and summer taxes? You two were close. So what? Big deal."

Seth swallowed hard and cleared his throat. "Okay. Years later, the bottom fell out of the housing market, and Bradford Sail Inn was refinanced with a balloon mortgage. When I almost lost the Inn to foreclosure, Whitt bailed me out by buying half, becoming a silent partner."

"I'll say. Get to the damn point."

"Well, I couldn't even sell the Inn. Whitt offered me a loan. I didn't want to take it, but I insisted on a partnership at the very least. For a long time, there were no profits to share, and he said not to worry about it. Things would rebound. It was a long-term investment and . . ." he looked at her, leaving the rest unsaid.

She sputtered as the unacceptable truth dawned on her in a rush. Upset was too mild a word for what was coursing through her now. "So, I inherited his half, unprofitable as it may be, which means I'm responsible for summer taxes?" Her voice began to rise, and she rose to her feet furious. She was sure fumes and plumes of smoke must be rising from her head. "That's why Monalisa wanted you to talk to me. You— by default—inherited *me*. Making me, what? A charity case?"

Seth stood face-to-face with her. "Look, I thought Whitt told you. I had no idea he hadn't."

"This isn't about Whitt. This is about what *you* didn't tell me."

"The hell it is. There's a lot you, Miss Independence, haven't told me either. For example, how *I'm* responsible for what *Whitt* didn't happen to mention to you?" Seth's voice roughened. "Moreover, *you* haven't told me what the *trouble* with Whitt is all about."

"My lawyer said I can't talk to *anyone* about my legal issues, like an internal gag order or something. Anything I say can be used against me or hurt me. If my mother was alive, and I wish she was, I couldn't tell *her* either. Plausible liability, deniability, and who knows what else. There's a whole bunch of other legal ramifications all designed for prosecution, potential forfeiture, frozen accounts—you name it—but Whitt died, so it's all on me. Neither Whitt nor you ever gave me any credit for managing life and my business acumen."

Seth's temper had clearly reached a boiling point, and he fought back, his arms windmilling as he appeared to struggle with his emotions. His body language would be comical if the issues weren't so critical.

"That's convenient," he growled. "And by the way, I didn't *inherit* you any more than I inherited a heartbroken kid. Janie needs me, and God only knows what else—braces maybe? But I do know this. I'll take her and her shaggy mutt any day. That's been a gift. Having Janie keeps me sane while Mal—"

Sloane was quick to interrupt his tirade. "What's your sister got to do with all this?" She could barely hold on to her self-control. The pre-crying sting burning her throat and eyes didn't stop her words from pouring out like a river of anger. A river of frustration. And a river of pain. "Good grief, don't tell me, on top of everything else, that Janie's Whitt's *lovechild*."

Seth appeared to be losing his cool now. "She's Mallory's child, and yes, she was conceived in love, but she isn't Whitt's. Her dad was killed in Afghanistan. Mal was a war correspondent embedded with his unit. They were in a convoy. She saw David blow up in front of her eyes. Shrapnel got her, too. Put her in a coma. So, yes, I took Janie, and I hope someday, somehow, Mal wakes up. So, if I *inherited* anything, it was love.

"True, you inherited half of Bradford Sail Inn, but we're making a profit now despite COVID. Whitt offered me a solution to my problems, and I took it. Why is it so terrible that

I help his widow? Why can't I repay *my* debt? Don't answer. I know. I have a *Savior Complex*. I can help Mallory and Janie, but I can't help Whitt's family when I *owe him?* Who the hell do you think you are?"

Sloane rocked on her feet as a tsunami of feelings flooded her.

Seth continued, his voice firm and serious. "Helping is what people who love each other do. I rescued Whitt, literally. He rescued me financially when I was losing everything."

A huge wave of emotions overwhelmed Sloane—nearly knocking her out yet again with too much in too short of time. Too much had been happening and was still happening, and it was all too damn much. And if she was mad when she arrived on Cape Cod—and she was—then she was frickin' furious now. With him. With Whitt. With God, God help her.

"I don't like surprises, and nobody wants to be an obligation, let alone owe summer taxes, Seth. So, save your *Savior Complex* for someone who needs it more. I don't want it. Don't protect me. Don't worry your head about it."

Seth's whole body tensed, clearly getting set to stomp off. "Fine."

Sloane wagged her finger in his face. "I was gutted when Whitt died, but I can take care of myself."

Then he jabbed a finger, stabbing the air between them. "It isn't *all* about you, Sloane."

Arms folded against her chest, she took a step back. "Oh?"

"It's about Joel. Whitt. Me. And *my* promise."

She raised an eyebrow.

Seth got in her face. "I made a promise, too. Not a *deathbed* promise like you did, but still a promise. A life-long promise as valid as yours. A, *if anything happens to me*, promise . . ."

Sloane wasn't having it. "*Go to Cape Cod, find Joe*, Whitt said. Why didn't *you* tell me everything when I first found you?" She was not about to let him just walk away.

Or waltz away.

Or run away.

Oh no, not Sloane. She wasn't done. No, she was just warming up. "All you had to do was tell me that I inherited half of Bradford Sail Inn. I'm no damn damsel in distress."

Seth's expression reflected his anger and frustration. He started to pace, raking his fingers through his hair and shaking his head. He turned to face her, his tone sharp. "You think it's that simple, eh? *When* was I supposed to tell you? When you shocked the shit out of me showing up at the pier — out of the blue no less. Hell, I didn't even know *you* were *Lonnie* until you announced you were my best friend's widow. Was I supposed to tell you when you gave your independence speech? After your soccer mom-to-widow spiel? Or when Joel nearly drowned?" He paced again, his arms akimbo. "When we went flying? Or maybe after we made love? Some afterglow that would have made. Mighty piss-poor pillow talk, eh?" Then he just stopped.

He straightened, turned his back on her, and threw his next words over his shoulder. "Lady, you've got your men mixed up. Whitt loved being your knight in shining armor, not me. Whitt made me promise. He begged, *If anything happens to me, take care of Lonnie. Promise me, Joe.* He clearly had a lot of *promise mes* lined up." He started to leave. Then he hesitated again and turned back, looking, if possible, even more pissed. "I didn't ask for any of this, Sloane. I have my own set of issues." He paused. "Ya know, I think you'd tell a good Samaritan to fuck off."

Seth strode away, his pounding steps on the wooden dock making the moored rowboats, skiffs, and sailboats bounce, upsetting the gulls sitting on the pilings. And truth be told, her as well.

Sloane sat down on the edge of the dock, dangling her feet above the choppy water. She pulled her hoodie closed and zipped it. She yelled to his retreating back—not sure he heard her but hoping he did. "Whatever. You know, the most painful betrayals didn't come from my boss or the reporters. They came from those I trusted the most, but I didn't expect it from *you.*"

Sloane felt her tears gather in her eyes and choke her. She recognized the sour upheaval in her gut as ugly sobs burst from her troubled soul. Now *she* distressed the sea birds, and with loud protesting squawks, they took flight. There was an uptick in the wind. The sky darkened like her mood. She stifled her sobs, causing her body to surrender to a big ugly cry.

Her thoughts and emotions tossing like the sea, she headed back to her cottage. *Thank God Monalisa insisted the kids have a sleepover. Joel doesn't need to see me fall apart like this again. Not again.*

Chapter Seven: Blowin' In the Wind

The sea winds had a chill to them, so Sloane headed inside. She changed into her flannel PJs and exchanged her dock shoes with thick warm socks. She wished she had some cranberry wine to drown her sorrows, but remembering her hangover last time . . .

The screen door opened, revealing Addie carrying take-out bags. "Hello, food's here and"—she held out a carton of ice cream—"Rocky Road. I come bearing two spoons and two lobster rolls that I was assured were *thee* best in Cape Cod. Which do we start with?" She held the bag of lobster rolls in one hand and the Rocky Road in the other, lifting each as she spoke.

Sloane sighed. "Tough call. Those *are* the best lobster rolls ever. So, move over, Rocky Road."

The rolls were nestled in plastic containers and were loaded with so much lobster that they couldn't lift them without making a mess. Instead, they grabbed knives and forks and sent their mouths to tastebud heaven.

The perfectly buttered and grilled rolls were to die for, but first, they had to dig through forkfuls of rich lobster pieces mixed with mayo, celery, and sweet oniony deliciousness to reach them.

Addie practically swooned with her first bite. "Someone should write an ode to the lobsters who gave their lives so we could enjoy these. We don't even need fries with this."

"Told ya so."

After filling their bellies with the succulent lobster and

licking their fingers clean, they cleaned up and recycled the plastic and wrappers. Addie changed into her PJs and returned with the Rocky Road in hand. True to her word, she brought two spoons and sat cross-legged beside Sloane on the daybed, facing the pewter skies and churning sea to share the carton.

Addie jabbed her spoon into the creamy delight. "Okay, girl, spill."

"I don't want to ruin this heavenly feast," Sloane said around a mouthful of bliss.

Lifting a spoonful, Addie said, "Okay. Let's dish about that hunky Joe guy. He has the hots for you, girlfriend."

Sloane felt the heat in her cheeks. "Not anymore."

"What? Something changed from five minutes ago? Last time I saw him, his eyes were eating you up. I have eyes and could see that . . . despite all the chaos around us. By the way . . ." She lifted another spoonful of ice cream. "Sorry 'bout how all that went down. I had it planned but . . ."

Sloane lowered her spoon. "That hunk is Seth . . . thee Seth." She had told Addie about her embarrassing encounter with Seth back in their college days.

Addie set her spoon aside. "It is not!"

Sloane popped another spoonful into her mouth. "It is. In the flesh. In Cape Cod."

Addie's brow came together, forming a tight V. "But you came out here to find *Joe*. What gives?"

"That's what I wanted to know when I first got here. Turns out *Joe* is Seth *Joseph* Bradford. Locals know him as Joe."

"Hmm. Well, at least he's not *Little Joe*."

"I wouldn't know," Sloane retorted, feigning innocence.

"As if. Dish. This is the part where you set your spoon aside and give me all the deets."

Sloane wanted to fan her flippin' telltale face and its twitching lip. "We're fighting, and I'm taking my blocks, putting 'em in my wagon, and draggin' it home along with my sorry ass after I polish off this decadent fare." She jabbed her spoon into the carton for another scoop of Rocky Road.

Addie leaned forward, excitement in her eyes. "It must have been good if you're already fighting."

Sloane looked at her best friend like the girl was certifiably insane. "Fighting is good? Did you miss the part where I said he's *Seth*? As in the *savior* who rescued little ole me from the big bad boozers?"

Addie rolled her eyes. "So what? Get over it. What's your problem?"

"Don't get me started." And then her too-long repressed tears burst like a water pipe, and in the flood, she gulped. "I'm a widow."

Addie gathered her in her arms, patting her back. "It's okay. You're okay. Whitt's ashes brought this to the surface, and that's a good thing. You've been fighting this for months. You need to let it out."

"Nooo . . ." Sloane sobbed. "It's bad. Whitt's gone, and I slept with his best friend. Whitt's really gone . . . his ashes . . . I'm so bad . . ."

Addie turned slightly, her arm still holding Sloane's shoulder. "As a therapist, I need to tell you your response is completely normal. It's called bereavement sex."

"You just made that up."

Addie crossed her heart. "I did not. It's a real thing. It's part of how the heart heals, affirming life, and adults usually do that by—"

"Screwing his best friend?" Sloane blew her nose into the tissue Addie thrust at her.

"That's not how I'd put it if you were a client, but yeah, it happens. A lot. You'd be surprised."

Sloane thrust out her hand and showed her wedding rings. Strangely, as things sometimes went in life, the sunlight caught her diamond, and it seemed to flare in the waning light like a frickin' beacon. "Not when you're m-m-married."

Addie rocked her. "Sweetie, you're not. You are a widow, and even widows have needs. And since when did you decide to be celibate? That was never a hang-up you had."

Sloane giggled despite her tears. "What am I gonna do with *Whitt*?"

"What do you want to do with him?"

"Kick his ass."

Addie looked thoughtful. "Ya still mad at him?"

"Are you frickin' kidding me? Of course, I am. He didn't listen. Didn't stay locked down. Didn't mask up. Didn't distance. Hell, he didn't even wash his hands much. Didn't think of us. Didn't vax. His death was completely preventable. He left me in a frickin' mess."

Addie grabbed her poncho. "Alrighty then. Get your shoes and a jacket."

"Why?"

Addie walked to the door. "We're going to kick some ash."

Sloane jumped to her feet, slid into her shoes, and zipped her hoodie. "Yeah. Let's do it."

Addie grabbed the package on her way out. "Come on, sista."

Sloane shivered because the temperature had dropped, the sun had set, and the guests had retreated safe and snug in their cottages. No one even had a bonfire, which seemed strange.

Most nights, folks congregated at the firepit, and several beach bonfires flickered along the beach, but no one was around. Not star gazers. Not lovers. Not children playing like most nights. No fishermen. No sunset cruisers. Not even Whaley was out. No, none of that was happening. Sloane could only assume the threat of a storm kept everyone inside.

They walked down the empty beach until only the moon

and stars lit their way. They stopped when they found the perfect spot where the waves gently washed onto the beach and retreated, only to do so again. No drift line debris, no briny low tide, no smelly fish, just the cool spray of sea foam and ever-present ocean winds that were picking up. They turned to face each other.

Addie asked. "This place okay?"

Sloane nodded, too choked to speak. *Hell yes.*

Addie unwrapped the package, lifted the box lid, undid the seal, and fiddled with something else before removing the plastic bag. She set it on the sand, stuffed the wrapping into the box, replaced the box top, and stepped back. "Ready?"

Sloane nodded, gritted her teeth, and kicked. Oh boy, did she kick. She unleashed a torrent of anger and pain, kicked the hell out of the bag, and then kicked some more. A low growl emerged as she sent that sad sack up and down the shoreline, up the berm, through the beachgrass, past the beach plums, and then back to the water's edge, where it finally broke apart. Clouds and puffs of ashes escaped its confines, catching in the wind. Powdery dust filled the breeze, dusting the sand and covering the sea. She kicked the hell she felt out of her system.

Trembling and breathing hard, she sank to her knees, wailed and screamed, and rocked and shook. The sea seemed to mirror her turmoil, roaring to shore and getting her knees as wet as tears streaked down her face. She doubled over with the pain and sadness of everything she and Joel had been through since Whitt's death, but the ferocity of her loss, well, that stilled and quieted within her.

Sloane's groans gave way to moans, her wails to keening, and her tears slowed to a trickle. And then the memory surfaced.

I was a hot mess. Anyone who saw me would think I was the epitome of grace, competence, and confidence. Indeed, I carefully cultivated just that image. I appeared to be a well-put-together woman in charge. Those who saw me would be fooled by my expensive blunt-cut hairdo, classic clothes, poise, and the way I held myself. However, at that moment I was not — at all. My façade gave the impression the world must be my oyster, but folks would be wrong — dead wrong. Inside I was a volcano.

I looked at the gurney.

Whitt wheezed. "S-So-Sor-ry . . .   our pl-1 -lan" — cough — *"Cape . . . Lonnie, promise meeee"* — wheeze — *"find Joe."*

Each pain-filled word tore from Whitt's undoubtedly tortured, raw throat and laboring lungs.

Sigh. The steam seemed to go out of him. I heard his words and could see every syllable was torture, each sound strangled. Down deep in my core, I knew. Knew as I drove him to the hospital with a raging fever and hacking cough. Knew as my body went into shock. Knew when my brain went numb. Knew before my husband rasped his last words . . . promise me.

He was as good as gone.

I could feel it in my gut, my soul, like a huge hole in the fabric of who I was. The hospitalist squawked, but I was no longer listening. Fear consumed me as they rolled Whitt to the Intensive Care Unit. My love couldn't help him. I couldn't save him, and neither could they.

Sloane deflated in a sad heap on the beach and said goodbye to her mate, her *husband*, weeping with all she had left. *Goodbye, my love. Goodbye, Whitt.* She hung her head, heard a huge splash, and looked up to see the silvery flash of a whale breaching in the moonlight. Another splash revealed her silver calf following her. And then another whale breached, and Sloane rose too. Lighting flashed as if her personal angst set it free, too. Were the breaching whales the signal she needed to let loose and go on? *A sign? To let Whitt go?*

She walked to Addie, who had witnessed her breakdown.

Addie smiled and draped her arm around Sloane as they returned to the cottage.

Sloane gathered herself, took a deep breath, and let it all

go. She looked Addie in the eye. "I kicked Whitt's ash."

They laughed when Mother Nature's storm roared, and they ran for cover.

Chapter Eight: Stayin' Alive

Sloane slept in the next morning. When she awoke, she stretched in the sunlight that streamed through the window. The trade winds greeted her by billowing the thin curtains. She trudged out of bed, smelled coffee—grateful for it—used the bathroom, poured a cup of coffee, grabbed some napkins, a coffee cake, and plates, then went outside to enjoy her morning view, blowing on her coffee to cool it.

Addie was already out there. "Mornin', sunshine. I see you're finally up and at 'em."

Sloane placed the coffee cake on the picnic table and gestured to it. Addie took a piece and bit into the cinnamon and yeasty cake.

Sloane grinned. "You bet." And ate some cake, too.

Addie smiled as she chewed, swallowed, and asked, "What's your plan for today? Any ass kickin' on the agenda?"

Sloan giggled. "I'm terrible." She sipped her coffee, broke off another tiny piece of pastry, and lifted it to her lips.

"Nope. You're grieving. Five stages and all that." Addie broke another chunk off.

Sloane sipped her coffee and paused. She waved her hand around. "I'm all over the map with my emotions."

Around another sip of coffee, Addie added, "The stages of grief aren't linear. And they're not in order either. They are what they are. Sad. Mad. Sudden. Prolonged. Eternal. Brief. And everything in between. You know loss. Remember when your mom died?"

Sloane chewed another bite. "I had Whitt back then."

"Now you have *you*. All grown-up you. And me. And Joel."

Sloane gave a soft smile. "Yeah, I do." She squeezed Addie's hand. "Thank you." She swiped a napkin across her sticky lips and sucked her fingers to get the last bit of frosting.

Addie smiled. "That's what friends do. They take care of you when you need it."

"That's what Seth said."

There was a bright light in Addie's eyes. She nodded. "I know."

"You do? How?"

"Why did you think I showed up bearing Rocky Road and two spoons? I think *everyone* heard the two of you. You guys got it bad."

Sloane dusted her hands off and shook her head. "No, we do *not*."

"I dunno." Addie's voice lilted at the end with a sing-song tone. "There was a lot of passion goin' on. Just sayin'."

"You think?" Heat crawled up Sloane's neck.

"Uh-huh. So, what's the plan?"

Sloane frowned and took a few minutes to think. "For the future or today? I gotta get outta here. I'm so embarrassed by how I acted."

"How about some sightseeing?" Addie suggested. "You said you were painting a new Cape Cod Lighthouse series, right? So, you need to see some lighthouses up close and personal."

"Sounds good. I'm up for it. Thanks for everything, Addie." Sloane gathered their breakfast remains and headed into the cottage. She pulled on some jeans and a t-shirt and headed to the kitchen.

Addie slipped on flip-flops and stopped her. "Sloane, there's only so much pain a soul can hold. You had to let it out. Plus, we solved a big problem."

As Sloane rinsed the coffee cups, she turned to look at Addie. "What problem?"

Addie winked and grabbed a dishcloth to dry the cups. "The problem of what to do with Whitt's ashes. That's solved."

They both doubled over, holding their sides, laughing so hard Sloane was afraid she'd pee herself.

"Oh my God, I'm a terrible wife. I'm so selfish. What if the others here wanted to . . . I don't know . . . have some sort of ceremony or something? I, uh, literally kicked his ashes to the sea."

Addie placed the coffee cups in the kitchen cabinet and chuckled. "Yeah. You could've been a kicker for the Detroit Lions."

Sloane paused, thinking for a few seconds. "I'm better at it than they are, that's for sure. But seriously. What if I should have, I don't know, put them somewhere special? Hold a memorial for the locals?"

Addie smiled, walked to the end table in the adjacent living room, and lifted a baggie, waving it back and forth. "I saved some."

Surprise had Sloane's mouth forming a huge O. "You did what?"

"Saved some ashes, just in case, you know, you needed a piece of ash."

Sloane gave her best friend a huge grin and winked. "Girlfriend, you rock!"

Addie linked her arm through Sloane's. "Get your sketchin' stuff. We have lighthouses to see."

Sloane grabbed her purse and a few art supplies, making sure she had her phone and keys, grateful that Monalisa had the kids launched for another day of *Captain Kids*. She joined Addie by the front door. "I'll drive. I know you must be tired from your drive here and all the drama yesterday. I've planned to hit three lighthouses. Feel free to tour them while I sketch and shoot some pictures."

The day was beautiful, the sky clear and dotted with cotton ball clouds, and the water as blue as the sky. Or maybe it was several hues of blues, providing a promising potential painting in her future. Sunlight bounced with the waves tinging their crests gold.

"First stop is Highland Lighthouse," Sloane announced. "There's supposed to be tours, a museum, and a gift shop."

Addie squealed when they passed Truro Vineyards. "We gotta stop there. Looks like fun. The sign says there's a wine-tasting tour."

Sloane couldn't help the memory of Seth planning a date for them there, but she said, "Another day, Addie. Can't risk doing a drunken sailor's routine right now. We're almost there."

"Aye aye, mate. I forgot you get horny when high."

"I *so* do not."

Addie adopted both a tease and a threat in her tone. "Oh, you *so* do. Want me to check with Seth about that?"

"As if. We're fighting at the moment. I don't want to think about him." But, of course, she *did* think about him anyway. How could she not? Like it or not, he did add some pep to her step, spice to her life. His appreciative looks, his silly jokes, and his attempts to rhyme, well, they added something quite nice.

Sloane couldn't continue that line of thought, though, because her GPS told her *Turn right in fifty feet, your destination is on the left.*

She drove past the Highland Museum, a two-story gray wood-shingled building, and turned into the parking lot a short distance from there. Just ahead of the lot stood the light-house and *keeper* house.

Addie bantered with her as they walked the path, her voice revealing her excitement. "Look at this place. I can't wait to get inside."

Neither could Sloane. As lighthouses went, it was spectacular, rising from green clifftop like a topper on a three-tiered wedding cake. The lightkeeper's house was spread beneath the 66-foot brick tower. The sunlight caught and winked as the sun hit the lens of the beacon. Sloane itched to climb it, but there was work to do first. She fought hard to curb her enthusiasm.

It was an easy walk to the entry, and she stopped to take pictures from every angle she could before joining Addie. When she reached the porch, Addie threw her hands out to the sides.

"Bummer. Look." She pointed to the door. The sign on it read *Closed for restoration and repair.*

Sloane sighed, then cheered up. "Look, there's another sign pointing to an observation deck up ahead."

They made the walk on the patchy path. Sloane couldn't describe it. It was easier to sketch than to define, but she took her cellphone out just in case. A few clicks captured its essence so she could paint it as accurately as possible. Then she laughed. *Who am I kidding?* She knew she'd add pebbles thrown in for visual contrast and texture interspersed with green scrub grass and sand. She typed *patchy, potholed, gravely, broken, cement, pebbly,* and *sandy* into the notes she kept on her phone.

Not trusting her new cell to function as it claimed, she typed the date and time so she'd have a record of the light at the least. Sometimes, she'd revisit sites to catch it at different times. She chuckled again because her imagination might turn it into sunset no matter what it was.

Her work was inspired by nature and imagination but not exactly reality. One of her best Michigan lighthouse scenes was a blend of several photos. She had taken snapshots of the lighthouse in bright morning light, a stormy afternoon, and a crystal-clear night. When she started to paint, she followed her artistic process as she always did. The final painting depicted the lighthouse in the dark of night with whitecapped waves in a stormy sea.

When she and Addie reached the observation deck, a boulder affixed with a brass marker detailed the lighthouse's history. She was shocked at how much the cliff on which it perched had seriously eroded. Scary thought.

The cliff was high, and a sign warned, *unstable*, but the view — my oh my — was spectacular and breathtaking. The sea looked like a sheet of sapphire. She couldn't start painting the lighthouse yet, but she could sit and sketch it from the observation deck benches. For good measure, she included a drawing of the marker. She'd already decided to use acrylics to depict the structure in as many moods as she could imagine, perhaps including the surging sea she had first fallen for at Race Point.

Her fingers flew across the pages as the wind teased hair from her headband, sending tendrils dancing. Her attention snagged onto a dried piece of sea grass skipping across the sand, pausing like a butterfly before it blew onto a bit of gravel to travel through the long beach grass. It didn't distract her for long, though. No, it gave her more to work with.

When she was satisfied with her sketches, she caught Addie's attention. "Next stop, Race Point, to see not one, but three lighthouses. I heard we hafta hoof it, so we'll need to get you some decent hiking shoes."

Addie pouted with a high-pitched whine reminiscent of their college days, her tone rivaling the wind through the ornamental grasses. "You didn't say anything about hiking. I don't feel like going back to the cottage to change. These will be fine."

Sloane smirked and teased. "Oh, but I did tell you."

Addie scoffed. "When?"

Sloane grinned. "Two minutes ago."

Monalisa had just left the office when Sloane walked through the Inn's arbor decorated with purple, white, pink, and blue hydrangeas.

"Hi, Sloane, feeling better? Over yesterday's shock, I trust? Where you off to today?"

Sloane gave her a rueful smile, hoping it was convincing. She wasn't sure of much lately. "To see, uh, three lighthouses at Race Point."

Monalisa smiled, nodded, and warned, "Better ride the bus. Save the twenty dollars to park at MacMillan's. Oh, and take water with you. And insect spray. There's some in the office if you don't have any. It's quite a hike to Long Point. Start at the end of Provincetown on Commercial Street and just keep going. Follow the dike. You've got good weather for it—another beautiful Cape Cod day." She stopped and glanced at Addie's feet. "Need to change out of those flip-flops. You'll never make the trek in those."

"Yes ma'am."

Sloane tittered.

Addie stuck her tongue out and headed for the cottage.

Sloane let her gaze roam the premises while waiting for Addie's return—not looking for Seth or anything, mind you. However, she spied Seth across the Commons, directing staff dealing with the problem of the deliveries from the day before. *Seems like he's fine as wine.* She shook her head and ordered herself to focus on her lighthouse plans.

Addie returned properly clad and carrying a backpack. Sloane led the way to the bus stop that was across the road. After a short walk, they sat on the weathered bench. She lifted a hand to shield her eyes from the glare of the sun bouncing off the asphalt, wishing she'd worn a hat instead of the red pirate bandana she'd poached from Joel's collection. They were chitchatting about their college days when the bus pulled up.

The digital sign across the windshield read *MacMillan Pier*, indicating it was the bus they wanted. Sloane deposited the two-dollar fare and found a seat for them. As they rode, she people-watched and enjoyed the easy comradery, soaking up the beach vibe tribe. Locals, she presumed, and tourists boarded along the way. All headed into Provincetown and the Pier. She wondered how many were hiking to the light-houses. Maybe she'd see some of them on their trek. Time would tell.

When they reached the terminal, Sloane admired the lei-surely island pace of the people milling about outside her window. It was so unlike the hurried frenzy at home.

When they exited the bus, the driver pointed in the direc-tion they needed to go. "Just down the street there, oceanside, not inland. You can't miss the trail. Between you and me, you only need to see two of the three lighthouses out there. Wood End Bar is *not* so conveniently located—many a ship got wrecked on that huge sand bar—it's literally at the end of the island. Looks just like its sister lighthouse, Long Point."

Sloane gaped in surprise. "No, I didn't. Good to know. Thanks." *Didn't Seth say something like that when we flew over the island? Ugh. Stop thinking about that man!*

The laid-back older gent beamed his appreciation. "Like I said, go to Long Point, and you've seen it all and save a mile's walk. You can see Race Point Lighthouse when you go on a Whale Watch." He winked and spoke in a stage whisper, "Dolphin *Whale Watch* is the best. Day's warming up."

Sloane nodded. "I think I saw it when Seth took us."

Even with the sea breeze, she could feel the heat. The blaz-ing sun lit the crests of the surging waves, making them spar-kle like a shiny new engagement ring. The sun was unbroken by any clouds or trees. She offered her signature *ta-ta* wave as she thanked the driver and led the way through the congested but festive tourists, pausing to permit a peddle-cab filled with passengers to pass by.

Many tourists were decked out, elaborately dressed and coifed. Some were members of the LGBTQ-plus community, others were just eclectic and possibly eccentric as well. She soaked in the colorful crowd and the tolerant vibe of the people enjoying the rich diversity in nature and human behavior.

The Provincetown *Causeway* trail, aka Long Point Dike, to the lighthouses was easy to find. Some called it a *jetty*, while others used the terms *break wall* or *dike*. It was made of concrete slabs jutting into the sea and over the beach, but there were gaps, jumps, water, and slopes to deal with or cross. It wasn't as easy as it looked online. However, it cut the walking quite a bit, or so they heard from other experienced locals they encountered along the way.

Once off the causeway, they hiked through the sand. The area wasn't labeled or called a strenuous walk, but it was long and wound through some mushy, reed-filled sections. They soon found themselves in ankle-high beach grass, slicing and stinging their lower legs. The trek seemed more than hard from Sloane's perspective. It was more challenging than she expected, and the sun pounding on them didn't help. She wiped the sweat from her forehead more than once, and they stopped several times for a swig of water. *Will we ever get there?*

Sloane readjusted her bandana and ran her hand through her damp bangs. "I think we may have bitten off more than we can chew." Her eyes were riveted on the weedy path, the contours of the sand, keeping free from stinging nettles, and how uncomfortable she was that she neglected to look skyward.

Their walk in the wild eroded Addie's usually pleasant mood. From what Sloane could see, Addie's girly-girl mannerisms were displaying her frayed nerves. Addie puffed her hair off her brow, stomped down some nettles, muttering curses under her breath, clearly on the verge of something not good — like a meltdown.

Sloane was just about to suggest giving up when she finally saw the square white brick lighthouse tower squatting ahead of them, "Wahoo! We found it." She sank to the sand, thanking her lucky stars. Had they turned back, they would have missed it, and it was literally right in front of them. She'd have been kicking her own can if they turned back. As it was, she wished they had run into a dune buggy so they could have hitched a ride. She was hot and gritty and sweating buckets. Surely she was dehydrated, despite the water she drank.

Addie slumped down beside her while Sloane, too tired to walk another step, pressed her camera phone on. She took picture after picture from every angle, even lying down. She recovered enough of her senses to see rusted bars on a rectangle window that had dripped orange and red down the surface of the gleaming white tower. A single-story small white building, its red roof shining in the hot sand, squatted behind the lighthouse.

She sketched them both and took notes. "I'm so glad the other lighthouse is identical. This must be the end of the world. How could another one be more remote than this?"

Addie appeared flushed and irritable as she shrugged. "To use a seventies term, *far out*. This lighthouse should be named Far Out Lighthouse."

"I think the guidebooks might call it that, but I'm not sure." Sloane was too exhausted to think straight.

Addie spat her next words in a firm tone. "First thing, when we get back, I'm going to grab an ice-cold beer. I'm not walking anywhere after this."

"Right there with ya, sista. Luckily we are not going any further. I'm all for returning and calling this mission accomplished." She shot her last pic of the tower, whose white bricks seemed to glow yellow and gold in the amazing light the area was known for.

No wonder Provincetown is a beacon for artists. "I can't believe this light. I've never seen anything like it. Nothing comes close. It's like being on the ocean in a boat with one side land and three sides open to the sea, creating this unbelievable, unbroken light. Sea light. Magnificent!" She twirled, looking skyward in ecstasy. "I'm in heaven. This here? Heaven on earth." Beat but ecstatic, she whipped the pirate bandana off and let her hair blow free. The breeze carried the scarf away, taking her troubles with it.

Addie ignored Sloane's rhapsody. "Whatever."

Chapter Nine: Leaving on a Jet Plane

Once Sloane and Addie dragged their sorry selves back to the pier, their first stop before boarding the bus was the *Sailing Pig* for a cold beer and some oysters. Truth be told, they each sucked down more beers than shellfish.

Addie sighed. "Girlfriend, I am such a city girl. Had I been one of those pilgrims who first landed here, I'd be the *dead* one. No wonder they left this site. It's hot and sandy and *dry*. But this beer here"—she raised her stein—"this beer is just dandy."

Sloane laughed. "I'll drink to that." She clinked her stein to Addie's. "Don't you just love the names of P-town's shops?"

Addie nodded and swallowed. "Listen to you sounding like a local. P-town, not Provincetown, huh? And who knew you were such a history buff, pilgrim's first landing site notwithstanding. Impressive. But I do love the shop names—*The Angry Tomato, Sailing Pig, Salty Dog,* and *Twisted Oyster*." She giggled. "Thank God we have a bus to take us home, or we'd be rightfully labeled *Tilted Tomatoes*."

Sloane rose from her rum barrel seat, leaned over the table, and playfully poked her gal pal's arm. "I've got it. The name for my place would be *Kick Ash Kitties* or *Sea Ho Bangsters*. Get it?"

"No."

Sloane put her hands on her hips, giving Addie *the look*. "Don't give me that. You *so do. Ash? Ho? Bang?*"

Addie huffed. "Speak for yourself. It was lame. Too much of a stretch. I'd rather have a *Wicked Weiner*."

The town hall steeple bell rang, letting them know it was six o'clock. "OMG, Joel! Gotta get home."

"Cool your jets, Mama. I happen to know Seth is taking them crabbing, and we'll return to a succulent beach feast. He's got them covered."

Sloane raised her brow. "Seriously? Who said that?"

"A certain little blue boy who's currently in deep do-do and is trying to reach a lewd lady so they can—how you say?—make nice." Addie waggled her eyebrows and made a kissing noise.

Sloane punched her. "Say what? Make out you mean?"

Addie shrugged. "Same diff."

But there was no making up, out, or love. The promised meal was there, but Seth was not. Instead, he was flying a Cape Cod Sunset Flight by Night Tour. Sloane groaned, turned to Monalisa, and asked. "Who writes those tour titles?"

"That would be Joe. Sometimes with Mallory's input, but ever since the accident, he's been—let's say very responsible for most things."

Sloane was curious. "What do you mean by *responsible*? Wasn't he always a knight in shining armor?"

A huge belly laugh burst from Monalisa. "That's rich. Grab some crab legs and take a seat. There's a lot to tell you about Joe. A lot you may not know. Boy Scout? Choir boy? Savior?" She humphed as she grabbed a plate for herself.

Sloane exchanged a look with Addie and wondered if her eyes had fallen from her sockets and if her mouth was hanging open, she was that floored. *Seth not a choir boy? How is that possible?*

After Janie and Joel were fed and ran off to play with a boisterous Whaley, after the last bite of tasty crab melted in her mouth, and after the sweetest corn on the cob was consumed, Monalisa handed her and Addie a cold brew. The three of them sat at the picnic table next to the fire.

Monalisa began telling Seth's story, and what Sloane learned floored her. It wasn't pretty, to say the least. Turned out he and Whitt got into and caused a lot of trouble in their youth. *Who knew?* Not anything illegal. Well . . . Seth had gone joyriding in a plane one time—okay, the plane wasn't his, and there was talk of jail. Certainly, a risky and potentially life-altering choice, but she got it.

Likewise, it appeared her calm and steady Whitt was frequently as untamed as his bro in tow and the instigator behind many of their pranks and parties. And between the two of them, there seemed to be more than taking risks physically . . . more than horseplay.

"You've no doubt heard of benign neglect, right?" Monalisa asked.

Sloane shook her head. "I've heard of neglect, but how can it ever be *benign*?"

Monalisa peered over her half-lens glasses. "It's benign when you choose your battles, know when to back off, accept kids will be kids and boys will be assholes, and look the other way. But when you go overboard with the blind eye bit, as Whitt's folks did, the kids will suffer real neglect. His parents often left him behind when their globetrotting days began. They figured the boys were high school graduates working summer jobs here at the Inn and in town, but sometimes boys take things a little too far and dive literally into trouble. That happened at Race Point Beach when Seth and Whitt went swimming despite the shark warning flags flying on shore, and Whitt got caught in the undertow."

Sloane nodded. After all, she knew the story but hadn't known about the shark warning flags. She also hadn't known about Seth's parents' divorce or how upset he became as a result, feeling abandoned and resentful. Nor did she realize he had not only experimented with drugs and alcohol but also shirked his responsibility, leaving the Inn overbooked and unmanaged. It all started him down a dubious path, and much of that could be laid at her Whitt's door.

"After the incident with Whitt, Joe wanted to fly to clear his head. He didn't have his license yet, but that didn't stop him. With an airport so close to home, the temptation was too much, so he *borrowed* a plane without permission. But flying when high, well, that leads to trouble. By some miracle, he talked his way out of it.

"He got his flight license as soon as he could, which was way too young to my way of thinking. As he grew up and matured, he got good enough to take flying stints and jobs around the country and frequented the air shows. Don't get me started. Never could tie him down in those days. The only tie-down for him then referred to parking his plane."

Sloane remained quiet, taking in all Monalisa said before she spoke. "I met Seth when I was in Ann Arbor going to college. He was my flight instructor. He thinks he rescued me, but I could have handled it."

Addie made a choking sound.

Monalisa raised an eyebrow. "Hmm. Could you have, though? Really?" Her gaze pierced Sloane's conscience, making her shift and chafe under the scrutiny.

Sloane briefly reflected on the memory while watching Addie chomp on her lower lip. Then she glanced at Monalisa and mumbled, "I thought so, then, but I guess I was damn lucky he *was* there. But the next day, I was recovering from the roofie—"

Monalisa's body jerked upright. "What? Wait. So, someone slipped you a roofie, and Joe got you before it got—literally—criminal, and you were mad at *him*?"

Sloane shrugged, throwing her palms out and waving

them in front of her. "Not my best moment. I was mad at *me* more than anything. Plus, I was mortified and half-naked. At the time, I just wanted to get out of there, crawl into a hole, and pile the dirt over me. Then I got called home to take care of my mom and never saw him again."

Addie piped in. "Until now."

Monalisa nodded. "All I know is that after Ann Arbor, Seth joined the Air Force and took way too many risks. Reckless and restless were how I'd described him back then, but once Mallory got hurt, he came home. When Brad, my late husband" — she paused, a shimmer crept into her eyes, then she cleared her throat — " died, Joe, well, he stepped up to the plate, ran this place, started Wing It, and the rest is history.

"Then Janie came into his life, and is it any wonder that he has a bit of a hero attached to his halo? But make no mistake, there are times when his halo dims and tips. He usually catches it before it falls off, though. At his core, he is a good guy with flaws, but aren't we all?"

Sloane thought about it as they walked to her cottage. She smiled. *Yeah. He is a good man.*

Monalisa paused by the door, taking a breath. "It wasn't until after Afghanistan that he grew up. His involvement — the strings he pulled — landed Mallory in a coma. That is not my story to tell. All I can say is he has been doing his penance ever since."

Addie looked like Sloane felt . . . shocked. "Wow. Just wow. Who'da thunk it?" She turned and entered the cottage.

Joel and Janie careened around the corner with Whaley in pursuit like they usually did each night.

Monalisa nudged her. "Walk with me." She led the way down the narrow walk until they reached the office. She entered and switched the light on. She held the screen door open and leaned outside to say, "I'll just be a minute more." She returned and held out an envelope.

Sloane cautiously took it. "What's this?"

Monalisa's foot tapped impatiently. "Open it up and take a look."

Mystified, Sloane used her finger like a letter opener and made a mess of the envelope. "This is uh, a check."

Monalisa nodded. "Uh-huh."

"Why would I get another check? I used the last one you gave me for taxes. Did I overpay?"

Monalisa shook her head. "No, taxes are paid. This isn't that."

Bafflement took over. "Huh?"

Monalisa smiled. "You sold a painting."

Sloane gaped, dumbstruck. "What! How? When?"

Monalisa looked her in the eye. "A wedding guest saw the painting, and Joe—"

"What's Seth got to do with this?"

Monalisa made a face. "He set the price and sold it on the spot."

Sloane shook her head. "He did not!"

"He did."

Sloane looked at the check closely. "This check has a lot of zeros."

Monalisa nodded.

"He saved my bacon." Sloane hesitated, then added, "Again. This feels like . . . I don't know . . . Another kind of hand-out."

Monalisa shook her head *no* this time. "Not even a hand up. This was a *sale* of your *work*. Don't you get it? You've saved yourself. You sold paintings at home and now here. You know, you and Joe are a lot alike. I think Whitt was right about that. You are a good match."

"What? Whitt said we were a good match? Ha! Goes to show you what he didn't know."

Monalisa winked. "Your promise to him sent you here,

right? Got you painting again? Got you that check."

Sloane's smile rivaled any champion anywhere. *Take that, Adrián, and shove it.* "Cape Cod got me painting again. And so did you."

"But Joe got you rolling—literally and figuratively. I saw your sketch of him first. Did you know that?"

Just then, Sloane's phone chimed, indicating a text. She looked at it. Samuel Blumfeld, her lawyer.

Urgent. Come home. Need to meet.

She tapped back her response.

K. How soon?

Now.

She sighed and then gasped. She could feel the blood draining from her face and her heart pounding against her chest. She suddenly felt hot, then just as fast, cold. She struggled to breathe.

Monalisa must have noticed her reaction. "What is it?"

"My attorney. We have to leave . . ."

Joel—in the middle of playing hide-and-seek—gave away his hiding place, bellowing at the top of his lungs. "Noooo! I'm not going. You can't make me." He stamped his feet.

Janie apparently heard Joel and emerged from a nearby tarp, joining the chorus. Whaley added to the fuss, and Addie came running down the walkway.

Monalisa placed a hand over her heart, patting her chest and looking shaky, too. "Lord have mercy. Settle down all y'all. Nobody's going anywhere." She took Sloane by the elbow and dragged her back down the sidewalk to her cottage, then pushed her inside, followed by the whining children and Addie. She only stopped to press Sloane onto a chair and mumbled, "Too damn much for you. Again."

Joel started yelling again. "We can't go home. Mister Joe said we'd go whale watching. And what about *Captain Kids*? We're having a pirate ship battle. And I haven't gone to the *real* beach yet or the Pirate Museum . . ." And finished with a whine. "You promised."

Sloane choked out, "We'll come back—"

"You promised. A promise is a promise."

Sloane put her face in her hands. *He has me there. Haven't I always said that?*

Addie made a half circle with her fingers, then stuck them in her mouth and blew a loud but piercing whistle that stopped Joel's barrage and quieted everyone else. "Sloane, go home. Take care of business. Joel will stay here with me. If need be, I'll drive him back after he finishes all the plans that have been made. You need to consult with your lawyer. That's that."

"I can't just snap my fingers and get on a flight home."

"You won't have to," Addie's quiet voice stated. "You fly yourself back home. Use one of Seth's planes."

Monalisa looked aghast but didn't protest or intervene. Didn't say it was a problem, or *talk to Joe*, or *no*. Sloane took that as consent, even though it wasn't Monalisa's place to lend.

Addie wasn't finished. "Leave Seth a note, file whatever you have to file, then come back." She shrugged. "It's that simple."

Joel nodded that he was okay with Addie's plan.

Sloane packed a bag, grabbed her purse, phone, and the travel tote holding her art supplies and sketchbooks, then grabbed a paper and pen.

Her note was brief and to the point.

Seth, Borrowed your bird. Will return. Promise.

She folded the note and left it with Monalisa. She hugged Joel, reminding him of how much she loved him and promising to return. She said her goodbyes and headed for the airport.

Sloane's nerves had thrummed, and her stomach had tied

itself in knots from the moment she even thought of using Seth's plane — without his permission. It left a sour taste in her mouth. Her stomach and heart seemed lodged in her throat as she removed tie-downs, conducted the walkaround, checked off the checklist, and taxied to the runway. All systems were good to go. She aimed for the center of the runway and began her takeoff. Once she got up to speed, she lifted the nose, pushed the throttle, and left the ground. The takeoff was smooth, but the updraft was tricky. She gripped the stick with both hands and made adjustments.

I can't believe I stole Seth's plane. I hope he does report me. It's a damned good thing he had me fly this solo several times. I haven't quite mastered the winds, but I know this plane. Thank God there's no fog to deal with. She didn't have time to think about anything else. She had to focus like never before to keep from crashing. No doubt about it, she was as unsure about this flight as everything else that had happened since Whitt's death.

When she looked down, she could see a chop to the sea. *I sure hope this wind doesn't make trouble for me. My stomach feels as choppy as that ocean.* She took to the air like a duck takes to water. For the first time in a long while, she was soaring and feeling liberated from her thoughts that tossed like broken glass in the sea.

Once she reached cruising altitude, she relaxed and let the thoughts, the uncertainties, and the future be. Just be. It was what it was. It would be what it would be. All she had to do was direct the rudder. *I'll do more when I know more. Right now, I'm going home. I'm rising above — pun intended — Seth petting my peeves. He did what he did without malice of any kind. Why couldn't I see that? I couldn't see the forest for the trees. Up here, it's clear down there, not so much. Flying relaxes me better than meditation. It lifts me in every sense of the word.*

It's so quiet, I can hear my soul singing. But why does it have to sing Baby Shark?

PART IV
THE PROMISE LAND

Chapter Ten: Separate Worlds

Seth was one tired cowboy. *Scratch that. Make it pilot.* The night flight tour usually ended at the Sand Bar and Grill, but he begged off this time, too worn out by the day's activities. He dropped off his passengers at the terminal and wished them a good night. On autopilot, he lined his plane to park next to his other three, but something was wrong. He knew he was tired, but there was a gap that shouldn't be there. *What the fuck. One of my planes is missing. Too late to report it now. Besides who'd believe it? They'd think I was drunk. Can't afford to let anything like that get around. It'd finish me and sink my business. I'll deal with it in the morning.*

He quickly completed his post-flight checks, secured the plane, and headed for the parking lot. He clicked the fob for his *Jeep*, glad to see *it* was still parked where he'd left it at least. He got in, started it up, and headed for home.

His cottage was quiet when he got there. Only the dim light from a small tarnished lantern was left to greet him. He could hear all the occupants—including Whaley—snoring. Despite the stress of his backward, upside down, inside out, going sideways day, he flopped down on his bed—still fully dressed—and went out like a light as soon as his head hit his pillow.

In the morning, Seth, Monalisa, and the rest of the Bradford Sail Inn's crew stayed busy dealing with the wedding, the wedding guests, and the visiting out-of-towners.

Seth was happy to see the caterers managed to make the

necessary week early adjustment to their schedule. The parents of the happy couple were responsible for the other accoutrements and wedding crap.

His staff's only responsibilities were to accept deliveries, clear the green spaces, allocate the efficiency units at Tradewinds, set up chairs and tables, and transport the principals using his fully wedding-decked-out beach buggy.

He spotted Beach Plum Florist handling the flowers. They appeared rattled, but that was not his problem. *Hell, at this point, I'd go online and become the officiant, but I checked with the reverend, and he's cool.*

His hard-pressed staff had the assistance of the church ladies, who insisted they were too blessed to be stressed. Seth wondered if they might share a little of the *Kool-Aid* they had access to.

Even Janie and Joel proved useful as they fluttered around acting like traffic cops, directing delivery personnel to the Commons. He got a chuckle out of Janie discussing how to get around the grounds.

Seth noticed Joel had confiscated some packing materials and designed what appeared to be a simple but useful map of the grounds. He even labeled sections with *Headquarters, Beach Side, Dock Side,* and *Ocean View* and was constructing signage for each area on the property. After the *Captain Kids* van came to take Joel and Janie to camp, Seth was more than happy to refer the delivery people to the children's map and resolved to use it in the future. *Why didn't I think of that? Seems obvious, duh, dude.*

Seth looked out to see Beach Plum Florist setting up the wisteria-wrapped arch near the docks on the beach. The string quartet arranged their equipment behind them on the pier. He wondered if they realized they would be accompanied by the sounds of surge, roar, and slap of the sea. *That's the only music I'd want, with perhaps a chorus of seagulls. I'd personally prefer a simple oceanside ceremony consisting of me and Sloane, the kids,*

Monalisa, and the preacher . . .

As he supervised the set-up procedure, he mentally created his wedding scene, including Mallory, Jake, Hank, and a scattering of close friends . . . He jerked to attention when the frantic bride started yelling and began dealing with handing her off to the nearest staff person. *Bridezillas aren't in my wheelhouse. Then . . . Why the hell am I thinking of Sloane and a wedding? She wants nothing to do with me, and I feel like shit served hot on a bun.*

Later that afternoon, the wedding that almost wasn't was finally in progress. It looked to become a smashing success—if you didn't count the fact that the reverend tested positive for COVID. Seth had to quickly dive into the internet to become ordained to legally officiate the marriage. He had grabbed a sports jacket to wear atop his cargo shorts, since there was no time to change into anything better.

The groom lost the ring and his cool. Well, he didn't lose the ring—exactly—he *dropped* it through the planks of the dock into the surf below.

The bride dove in and retrieved the ring, raising it and saying, "Ta-da!" She seemed unfazed by the fact that she was dripping wet.

The groom looked ready to hurl himself into the water as well.

"Drinks on me," the father of the groom joked. Funny because the entire beverage expense for the event was on him.

What a story! *I wish Sloane was here to see this.* Then it hit him. He hadn't seen her the whole day. *Strange.*

Out of the corner of his eye, he spotted the arrival of a bob of seals swimming near the pilings, no doubt looking for cast-offs. Seals were curious animals but usually didn't frequent this beach. They were common off Race Point and always near the fishing boats at MacMillan Pier, but it was surprising to see them here.

Seth was much too busy to do more than note their presence. When his officiant duties to the bride and groom were finished, he permitted himself to open a bottle of rum and drink up.

He heaved a sigh of relief when the happy couple finally took off for their honeymoon on Martha's Vineyard and were no longer his problem. He graciously let the last of the revelers have some time to wind down the party.

What was left of the wedding crowd buzzed with excitement, danced, and chatted for a while longer, then began drifting away. Some went to their Bradford Sail Inn cottages, some hitched a ride with the wedding buggy to Tradewinds, and others embarked for God only knew where.

Janie and Joel behaved like they always did, running here and there, playing tag or whatever, with Whaley tagging along as usual.

Monalisa was supervising the catering staff as they cleared up the remains of the event. She took the hubbub worse than usual and seemed somehow *off* to him.

Seth directed the tear-down team to *stand by.* He was torn from his musings by a shout.

"Seal! Come look!" a lone wedding guest yelled from the marina about a hundred yards from where Seth was standing.

A few tired adults still in their wedding finery heeded the call and headed back to the dock. Seth followed along, joining Monalisa and the kids, watching the seals and enjoying their antics. He was still baffled by their appearance. *They're so far from their usual hang-out spots. It's unusual, but nothing about today has been remotely usual.*

Janie and Joel watched for a while until one seal swam out

too far to make watching easy, and the other wasn't doing much. The kids left to join their group of friends who played together each evening.

Monalisa began to walk away as the sun started staining the sky in brilliant golds and oranges, but she swayed, lost her balance, and fell into the ocean. She screamed, "Shark," just as one of the seals shot straight up like a rocket.

Many folks came running, grabbing whatever they could to help. Hank came too and picked up a boat hook.

Seth didn't know if the shark would mistake Monalisa for a big seal, but it veered toward her. In a heartbeat, he dove into the water to help Monalisa fight off the shark. "Hank, help!"

He socked the shark in the snout, then pushed Monalisa to the low landing deck so Hank could heft her out. He was in the process of getting out himself when a terrible pain hit him. "Fuck! It bit me! Help!"

Hank used the boat hook to pummel what appeared to be the shark's head.

Seth gripped the dock planks and yelled, "Poke its eye, Hank."

Hank thrust the boathook into the shark's eye, and it retreated, taking the boathook with it. He helped pull Seth onto the landing, carefully lifting as much of the injured leg as he could get hold of. He yelled over his shoulder. "Addie, call nine-one-one."

Seth's foot and leg looked bad. There was a lot of blood. It looked like his foot was barely hanging on. Hank wrapped up the bloody mess with his shirt and fashioned a tourniquet using his belt.

Hank patted Seth's shoulder. "A guest is tending Monalisa. She's gonna be fine."

In no time, a helicopter showed up to airlift Seth and Mona to Cape Cod Hospital. The pain would have brought him to his knees if he wasn't already on his back. He heard the din of voices but couldn't make out what was said.

Then someone said, "Fifteen ccs of morphine. Stat."

Addie almost panicked when Janie and Joel came running to the scene, yelling and screaming, clearly upset by what was happening. She took the kids under her wing and led them to a nearby picnic table after the helicopter took off. Using every tool in her counselor kit, she tried her best to calm their concerns, comfort them, and answer their questions. Both children were traumatized, and she had very few answers. After a while, they both quit talking and started shivering.

Joel started rocking. "I want my m-m-mom." Then he screamed, "Daddy!"

Addie put herself in the middle of them both. A kind guest grabbed a beach blanket and placed it around them. Addie swallowed and nodded her thanks. Her eyes brimmed with tears. She was in charge now.

Sloane landed the plane at Coleman A. Young International Airport, a small general aviation airfield close to her home. Once she arranged a parking spot and secured the plane, she called for a ride share to take her directly to her attorney's office. She had a late afternoon appointment.

When she checked her phone, she saw no new messages, but her battery was low. She couldn't do anything to charge it, though. She was leery of the car service that showed up, but the name and the information checked out, so she sat in the back with her duffle and tote bags and gave the driver the address.

Her lawyer was located in a picture-perfect upscale but not pretentious tree-lined low colonial office building on Mack

Avenue. She entered the classic black door with a bronze nameplate saying *Blumfeld, Goldberg, and Schiff, LTD Attorneys at Law.* A pert, well-dressed clerk invited her to sit in the traditionally furnished but functional waiting room, asking if she would like water.

"I would, thanks."

Sloane accepted the chilled bottle of natural spring water and monogrammed coaster with a smile. It wasn't long before Sam came out to walk her back to his office. His fit frame looked good in his tailored blue pinstripe suit, but his smile did not reach his eyes. He sat behind his massive mahogany desk and invited her to sit in a firm armchair on the opposite side. Two chairs faced the desk, and she took the nearest one.

Sloane was wired, tired, and tried to take a deep breath but failed. It got stuck mid-breath, and she coughed into the crook of her arm.

Naked alarm appeared in Sam's eyes. There was a 5th COVID surge running through Wayne County, Michigan.

"Excuse me." She paused, recovering. "I'm vaxed and boosted and haven't had the virus or any variation. It's nerves. I have a mask if you'd like me to wear it."

"No, that's fine. I've had my shots, too."

"Sounds like we're dog owners assuring people that our dog is vaccinated."

Sam gave a small grunt. "So far, our vaccinations are working. Until they prove otherwise."

When she didn't smile, he said, "Sorry, occupational hazard. My pragmatism and experience. I get paid for spotting problems."

He opened the file in front of him and set a yellow legal pad next to it, writing her name and the date at the top of the page. Then he steepled his hands, swallowed, and spoke in a firm businesslike tone. "You need to know this case is complex. I need permission to bring on another forensic financial analyst to uncover what the heck Whitt had going on. Whitt apparently used him in the past. I've also ordered an autopsy."

Sloane jolted, confusion running rampant in her brain. "Excuse me? It's been done already. Whitt died of COVID. There should be a record somewhere. Will the death certificate do?"

This time, a small smile crossed his face. "No, a *financial* autopsy. I've already uncovered shell companies, Cayman Island accounts, and more, but it's complicated. I need more help if we are to beat this thing and avoid prosecution, seizure of assets, fines, liens, forfeitures, and the like. Possibly even federal court."

Sloane froze as alarm and shock spread throughout her body, and she gasped.

Sam noticed. "That's why you have me and my friend, who can sniff all this out. In the preliminary consult I had with him, he thinks there may be a secret partner, a very silent partner. I don't want to get your hopes up, but . . ."

Sam blathered on for two hours of legalese. Sloane felt dizzy and confused, like when she had her income tax done or met with a financial planner or insurance person. *Pay Attention! Tuning this out is not an option. Boring goes with the territory. This is serious. Prosecution? Get with it. Haven't you learned anything?*

Sam glanced at her, obviously noticing her glazed-over expression. "I know that's a lot to digest. Trust me. That's why you have me."

Sloane straightened in her seat, anger taking over. "That's exactly what Whitt said, and it landed me in this mess."

He made a small harumph. "Yes, uh, I know, but trust—"

"Let me say it. Trust you, you're an attorney. Pardon me while I laugh."

Undeterred, Sam continued. "Moving forward, get a job, establish yourself. Be careful. Phones can be tapped. While it might be tempting, I must stress again, don't talk about this with anyone." He gave a half-smile. "Hope for the best and prepare for the worst."

Sloane shook her head. "I feel like I'm in a foreign country and don't speak the language. A bomb has blown up my life. I guess I'll just have to get it together, won't I? How do I support myself when Whitt cost me my art contacts and job? How do I go on?"

For the first time, something she could not identify shone in Sam's eyes, and perhaps something more than hope straightened his spine. Pride? Skill? She wasn't sure, but it made her feel better.

Sam nodded. "There are some documents that need your signature. Our notary will notarize them, and I can get things underway. We need to make our move before the opposition does. Proactivity is the best defense. That's my motto."

Sloane signed not on the proverbial line but where the red arrow sticky pointed. It felt like buying a house. A signature here, initial there, here a signature, there an initial . . . rinse and repeat.

Sam continued. "I've been reviewing your financials, and they are on the up and up. So far, it doesn't look like he cluttered *you* up. There are concepts out there we can check into to help you. The prosecutor may back off since they usually go for the win. I can try for forfeiture of wrongdoing. It may apply here. There's also abnegation."

She looked at him blankly.

"Look, it's late, and you're overwhelmed by all this mess. Prosecutors don't go after crimes they can't prove. We're protecting what we can. Your grandmother left you the house, and they may not be able to touch that. We're looking into marital assets. It sounds cold, but Whitt's death may help you . . . Like I said. I'm a good tax attorney. I got you."

Sloane asked to use his phone. "Mine's dead. I need to call the ride share. When will we be done with this case?"

"The case can take two to four—

"Four more months?" Shock drove her voice up an octave.

"Years."

Sloane gaped and then closed her mouth and stared at him for a long time, trying to wrap her mind around dealing with this mess for *years.*

"You live out on Lake Shore Drive, right? I can drop you off if you'd like. It's on my way."

She finally managed a nod. "Thanks."

Sam went on as if she were still listening. "We may have a third-party owner of assets, not joint ownership. That will help. Be patient." He led her out the back door, where his jet-black *BMW* waited.

It became apparent that Sam was all talked out, too. He remained silent and turned on his classic rock playlist, and Sloane was fine with it. He drove her to the side entrance of her house, and she made her goodbyes, knowing he'd keep her apprised of things. There was no more to do, nothing more to discuss.

She didn't understand why her signatures were so important that she'd had to rush home, but she was no lawyer. No, she was a single mom doing her best and making the best of what her rat bastard spouse made of her life. She was still angry. With Whitt. With the law. With life. With herself. With Seth.

She entered her house, and though a glass of wine, a cocktail, or a hot bath sounded good, it wasn't what she needed to clear her mind. She made her way through the kitchen and down the hallway to the living room, deciding to take a look at the work she had done in Cape Cod. As she flipped through her sketches, she found as many done of people as seascapes. She had countless drawings of Seth. It seemed to be her default.

Give her a pencil or charcoal stick, and out popped Seth.

Good looking, sad looking, pensive, joyous, surprised, tender, mad. You name it, she had drawn it. Several showed him battling the sea.

Sloane recalled using the sea as a metaphor for herself in the sketches. Perhaps Seth was battling on her behalf. She hadn't seen that then, but she was getting the idea now. *Guess my subconscious knows me well.* She sighed. *I guess I really am a tough nut to crack.*

Joel featured prominently in plenty of the sketches. And of course, Whaley. She was dying to paint these, but the one drawing of Seth and Race Point called to her the most.

Sloane mounted the steps to her studio. She turned on the light, praying she could represent all she had on her sketch pad using acrylics. She set up a canvas, prepared the paints, and started her work, slipping into her zone as she did — her highly productive place where everything disappears except the painting before her.

The temperature in the studio became stifling, and she wished the restorative sea winds of Cape Cod were billowing her curtains. The lake breeze was nice, but there was no salt in the air, and it dripped with humidity that glommed onto her body. She turned on the ceiling fan and shut the window, pretending Lake St. Clair was Cape Cod Bay.

Her brush raced across the canvas as she painted a scene where the sky and sea paired, nearly married. She used green, blue, and black brush strokes to portray them. She worked her best to reproduce the sound of those waves surging in and slapping the shore with their fury. She attempted to capture the proper light outlining the tall silent man with the pseudo-trade winds ruffling his hair and shirt, which was open to the elements, revealing a strong chest. A strong man. She meticulously rendered the yellow-white lightning branches spreading like a root system against a darkening sky.

Sloane tried to find the colors that could make the open mouths of the gulls *look* like their cries. She painted them in low flight, almost bouncing off the waves with wings spread wide. The roar of the strong storm winds was tricky to capture on canvas, as was the tang and bit of the salt air and the scent of the purple beach plums with their brilliant blossoms.

As a final touch, she decided to add the squat square Wood End Lighthouse standing amid the green scrub grasses bent by the wind. She carefully detailed the erosion fence in a warm brown, using sandy brown for the beach to contrast the cobalt sea and adding thin white lines lacing the shoreline.

She stepped back and sighed, satisfied with what she'd created. She sank to the floor and finally let loose her torrent of emotions.

Seth was not at her side, but he was in her thoughts, and surprisingly, in her heart. She missed him with all she had. Missed his rugged good looks and his hard-to-admit, mostly solid character. She didn't care any longer about their embarrassing past or whatever was in his past.

She remembered the time he got down to Joel's eye level and told him he would share the things his dad liked to do as a boy. And she recalled him conducting a pirate sword fight with Joel and Janie using driftwood from the marsh at Uncle Tim's Bridge.

Her thoughts turned to the way he'd run a hand through his dark hair, how she loved the wink he'd throw her way, and how she even appreciated his corny jokes and insane challenges. Her defenses were beginning to soften. *Am I so scared of my future that I won't accept his help? I'll let my attorney help, but not Seth? How does that make sense?*

Sloane had no idea how long she stayed on the floor but must have fallen asleep. She woke to the pounding sound of thunder. *A storm must be blowing in.* She couldn't hear any rain or wind and saw no lightning flash through the curtains, but the rolling thunder was clear. She slowly rose from the floor and stumbled to the window. Still, her legs were under her, and she was *up* at least.

Raising a hand to her forehead as if she could brush away her brain fog, she pulled the curtains apart. She felt so out of whack, like she was out of body or in a trance. She saw blue and red lights flash, heard pounding on her front door, and realized it was the police. *Police! Good God, what fresh hell awaits?*

CHAPTER ELEVEN: COME ON NOW, RESCUE ME

Sloane disarmed the home security alarm that she had installed after Whitt died and opened the door part way, the chain lock still engaged. These days, you just never knew how you could be hacked, jacked, smacked, or worse.

She stared at two Grosse Pointe Park police officers responsible for the pounding. One was a tall woman, the other a slightly shorter younger man, both dressed in their uniforms. They held their badges out so she could see their credentials. The photos matched their faces, but she didn't relax.

"Are you Sloane Wentworth?" the man asked.

"Yes. What's this all about? What's going on? Is everything all right?" *Stupid question, Sloane, would they be here if things were peachy-keen?"*

An automatic sensor suddenly switched on a low light in the kitchen, drawing the officers' attention beyond her past the darkened foyer. They responded to the light by tensing up.

The female officer asked, "Is anyone else here with you? May we come in?"

Sloane looked at them carefully as she considered their request. She cast her glance around and then moved to unchain the door to let them in. She led them into the den at their right, preceding them and turning on a desk light, trying to fortify herself for whatever they had to tell her. "I'm alone. Did something happen to my son?"

The officers entered cautiously, eyes alert.

Do I offer them a seat? Do I sit? Why am I thinking of etiquette now? But she knew why. She was trying to deflect, to divert them from whatever they were going to tell her. Her body and mind became hypervigilant, adrenaline shooting through her system, preparing her for the blow their words might deliver.

The young man, a rookie perhaps, answered her query. "Not that we are aware of. We're here to conduct a welfare check. Seems you haven't been in contact with, uh, your contacts."

The female officer asked, "Are you okay? Are you hurt? Ill? Is anyone endangering you?"

Sloane raised a hand to her chest. "I'm fine. I'm not ill. Why do you think I'm in danger?"

"Just following protocol for the welfare and wellness check, ma'am. You flew in today?"

Sloane's heart started beating so hard she was sure her heart was about to fly out of her chest. *Are they going to arrest me? Has Seth pressed charges for taking his plane?* "Yes. I flew in to meet with my attorney."

The officer opened a small notebook and flipped a page. She looked down at it. "Samuel Blumfeld?"

She sank into an armchair. "Yes."

"The flight went okay? No problems?"

Sloane cleared her throat. *Keep it simple. Just answer the question. Don't volunteer anything. You can call Sam if you need to.* She would follow his directives to a T. "No problems."

"Is it okay with you if we just look around? Make sure no one is here threatening you?"

"Be my guest."

The officers gestured to each other. One went upstairs while the other covered the first floor. The word *clear* kept repeating as they went from room to room. She wondered if their guns were drawn. *I'm watching way too much CSI.*

They returned to the den, and the woman asked, "Where's

your phone, ma'am?"

"It's here somewhere." Sloane looked around, glancing from her purse in the kitchen to the pockets of her pants. Her hands felt for it but didn't find it. She glanced at her purse again. "It's probably in the kitchen."

"Do you mind checking, ma'am?"

Sloane rose. "Of course not." She didn't find it charging on the counter as she hoped. She rifled through her purse and lifted it. "Found it." She wagged the phone in the air so they could see it.

"Is it charged? Would you check it, please?"

She checked, stared at the dead screen, and felt her face flame. "Apparently not."

"That's why it went straight to voice mail and worried your friend." The officer glanced at her notes. "Adelyn Springfield. She called us when she couldn't get ahold of you. We suggest you charge it and call her as soon as you can. We're glad you're okay, and be sure you lock up. Sorry if we upset you."

"No problem. I was working in my studio and zoned out . . . just fell asleep. It was an exhausting day, and I forgot to plug in the phone. I'm fine."

They radioed someone as Sloane escorted them to the door and set the alarm. For the first time ever, she felt very, very alone. She wished Whaley was around to cuddle, but her heart knew she truly wished for Seth instead.

Her stomach growled as she plugged in her phone, so she made a fried egg with a cheddar cheese sandwich. She washed it down with a glass of Chardonnay. It was an odd combination, but if people could have Mimosas for breakfast, she could have wine with her breakfast-dinner meal.

Sloane jumped when her landline rang. She seldom used it and had almost forgotten she had it. She took the call and wished she hadn't after hearing Addie babble that Monalisa had a heart attack and Seth was in surgery from a rescue attempt and shark bite.

"What are you telling me? What do you mean? Heart attack? Surgery? Shark bite? Hold on." She staggered to the wastebasket and lost her dinner. She mopped her face with a cool dish towel, rinsed her mouth, and tried to answer Addie's frantic screams.

"You okay? Sloane? Answer me."

Sloane's head swam with a million questions. "Where are you, Addie?"

Addie quickly reassured her. "I'm at the cottage with Joel and Janie. And Whaley of course."

Sloane sagged to the floor, extending the old-fashioned spiraled phone cord to its limits. "Is Joel okay? How is he?"

"He's quiet, but he's safe and all right. This has been a shock. We're spending the night at their place. I'm getting some of Joel's stuff now. Whaley's doing a good job comforting both kids. I'm going to start a fire, put on a movie, and we're gonna cuddle. I'll tell him I got ahold of you. That'll help."

"I'll call. Give me the number. My phone's charging. I'll use this landline. Tell him I'm flying back there at daybreak. Where are Seth and Monalisa now?"

"They were flown to Cape Cod Hospital in Hyannis. Monalisa has been treated. She's in the hospital cardio wing. They put in three stents. Seth is still in surgery for his shark bite. It bit his calf and foot."

"I think there's an airport in Hyannis. I'll check. If so, I'm going there first. If I'm lucky, I'll land by noon tomorrow."

"Call me. And for God's sake, keep your phone charged."

Sloane emitted a small sound, something between a laugh and a sob. "Yes, ma'am." She hung up and decided a hot bath and a cold glass of wine would help calm her nerves. She started with the latter and called Joel.

Janie picked up. "Bradford residence, Janie Armstrong speaking."

Janie's an old soul. So grounded. Sloane spoke using a gentle tone. "It's Miss Sloane. How are you doing?"

In her mind's eye, she pictured Janie's lower lip trembling, but her voice betrayed little of the shock she had been through. "We have had a devil of a day—"

There were sounds of two children grappling with the phone. Complaints abounded.

Joel whined, "Gimme. It's my mom."

Janie remained firm. "My house. My phone. My rules."

Joel grumbled his response. "Fine."

Janie talked a tad about Seth saving Monalisa with a quiver in her voice and then must have handed the phone over to Joel.

Joel muttered. "Can I talk to my mom now? Finally."

Sloane heard grumblings, but apparently, the phone was in Joel's hands.

"Mom, Seth got bit by a shark. There was a seal . . . Miss Monalisa had a heart attack. It's scary." His shaky voice almost broke her heart.

Sloane agreed but had to be strong for her baby. "Man alive, that's a lot to handle, eh, bud? But all the grown-ups are safe now. Are you okay?"

He must have nodded because she heard Janie yelling in the background.

"We got Whaley and Miss Addie to be with us. Tell her."

"Come back, Mama."

"I'll be there after lunch. Don't you worry."

CHAPTER TWELVE: I'LL BE YOUR SHERO

After Sloane ended the call, she needed more than a cold Chardonnay and a hot bath. Her emotions, thoughts, and prayers were tossed and turned like shells in the sea. It was hard to keep the images flashing through her mind of sharks, Seth, and Monalisa from completely sinking her boat.

She envisioned a scared Joel, sweet Monalisa's frail frame, blood — there had to be blood — Seth in surgery, and her soul bled. Finally, she grabbed her rosary and must have fallen asleep. It was hard to tell. Her inner voice seemed to be narrating her prayers automatically as if on a loop. All she could make sense of was Seth, Joel, and Monalisa.

And then, all of a sudden, the scene shifted, and Whitt was standing in front of her, saying, "Trust me . . . trust me . . . . everything's all right. It's fine. All good from here on out."

When Sloane woke the next morning, she took a hot shower, forcing herself to settle down and think straight. She made coffee, scrambled eggs, and toast for the nutrients. She also needed carbs, so she snuck in a Toaster Pop, its sugary strawberry deliciousness soothing her soul like nothing else.

Once she gathered everything she needed, she called the ride service and headed back to the airport. Whereas she'd been uncertain about the future the night before, that morning her focus was clear. Maybe Whitt's words in her dream were a sign, a message spoken to her subconscious, but it helped her decide three things. One, she was going to survive to rescue herself and Joel. Two, she was going to help Seth. And three, let him help her.

Sloane's anger with Whitt shifted for the better. Yes, he had messed up, but maybe some hope existed somewhere in all the chaos. After all, Whitt had been many things, but he *wasn't* a cold-blooded crook at his core.

Was he stupid about COVID? Yes. Too busy with work? A given. But at heart, he had loved them and was sorry for his mistakes. He'd said so in the end and pointed her to Cape Cod, where she could start again and learn from *Joe*.

As she thought harder, she did remember Whitt saying, "Good thing Joe didn't meet you first, he'd be good for you. You'd be like book ends."

She smiled, remembering Monalisa telling her the same thing.

Maybe Whitt knew she'd find what she needed in Cape Cod — new material to paint and help along the way. Perhaps he was somehow straightening things out from the other side of the veil between life and the afterlife. Her attorney suggested as much when he talked of a silent partner and the security from forfeiture of her inheritance from her grandmother.

Sloane's paintings were selling, and she had all sorts of material to work with to paint several new series — a Cape Cod series, a Lighthouse series, a Sea Breeze series . . .

First things first. Sloane grabbed her charged cell phone and called the hospital in Hyannis. She found Seth was listed in temporary critical care. She clung to the *temporary* part.

Once she got to the airport and completed all the necessary checks, she took to the sky. When she reached a cruising altitude, she put the plane on automatic pilot so she could think.

Sloane's thoughts turned to Seth. She'd found evidence in her sketches that she had become completely besotted with Cape Cod and its people. Especially with the man who introduced her to Race Point. Was that where she fell in love with him?

Perhaps her brain hadn't accepted it yet, but her heart and body had. When she'd painted the night before, she learned that she had memorized the tang in the air that clung to Seth's skin so that every sight, every detail of him and Cape Cod was now a part of her memory of the man he was and of the space and place he loved. Sea and sky.

She was of the sky and sea as well. Somehow, Seth became part of her, her heart, her soul. She recalled his devotion to Janie as he tried to braid her hair. She envisioned him flying kites and teaching Joel.

From their lovemaking in the paint mobile to the walks at low tide, to the savory clambake, to their mile-high flight circling the island, to the tang of the cranberry wine he introduced her to, he had become part of the moments she had etched within her heart. She remembered the rich lobster rolls they grabbed on the fly, their early mornings just sitting outside enjoying the sea breeze. She replayed mental tapes of Whaley's knocking them in the drink and Seth's sheltering arms steadying her until she regained her footing. She had incorporated all that into what made her happy. Seth had shown her what she needed to heal. It was his turn to heal now, and she was just the woman to help him do it.

After landing, Sloane rushed to the hospital only to learn they wouldn't allow visitors yet. Their COVID policy hadn't budged much from the early days. The doctors told her Seth and Monalisa had to recover and do physical therapy as they recuperated before they could go home. The hospitalist planned for homecare, and Addie's background helped with many of the details. *What a Godsend she is.*

After landing the plane in Provincetown, Sloane conducted the exit checks and walkaround and secured the tie-downs after refueling. She went into the terminal to check Seth's flight schedule and took a picture of it on her cellphone. She decided to make a *Gone Fishin'* sign for the kiosk. She knew she could manage the flights Seth had booked but was relieved that no *Flight by Night* tours were scheduled for the next week.

Sloane planned to fly Monalisa and Seth home if the doctors okayed it. For now, she was anxious to return to the Inn to see her son.

Within minutes, her wheels crunched on the gravel parking lot. From the looks of it, the kids were flying kites on the beach. She walked to the shore knowing the beach was more than a place, it was a feeling of being welcomed back to where she belonged.

Although she felt like running to gather Joel into her arms, she knew he didn't want her to baby or cradle him like she needed to. *Lord only knows what he saw, what he's feeling.* He needed to feel safe and secure. Able to take life as it comes. So while she didn't run, she did quicken her pace.

Whaley spotted her first and nearly tackled her as he welcomed her home. Joel gave her a happy wave but continued to fly his kite. A part of Sloane wanted him to fly into her arms, but he was too old for that kind of embarrassing reunion. Despite recent events, he appeared to be okay.

The wind shifted, the kites fell from the sky, and *then* Joel came running for her. She bent down and swung him up and around. Janie joined them with a hug of her own. Both children looked well, normal, and no worse for wear. Addie brought up the rear, retrieving their kites along the way. *What a champ. Way to go, sista.*

Sloane hugged Addie and exchanged info regarding Seth and Monalisa's homecoming. Seemed like the hospital and doctors had plenty to say about that. Medical transport would be bringing them back to the Inn. Monalisa would arrive back home in a few days, and her home care personnel were already scheduled. Seth would be brought home shortly thereafter. The hospitalist coordinated their respective arrivals to give the caregivers time to prepare. Addie said their cottage had been examined, and all obstructions were removed. No tripping hazards were left—apart from Whaley, whose ears picked up when he heard his name. Then he cast his eyes down as if he had messed up, whining and flashing his puppy eyes.

"Monalisa will need a walker just in case and just for a while," Addie said. "The big guy? He'll need a wheelchair. And crutches."

Sloane groaned. "That is going to make him a grump. I don't think he'll make a good patient. He's not a patient person."

Addie smirked. "I think you test his patience."

The ragtag family held a dinner-by-food-truck celebration for Sloane's homecoming and their reunification. Addie and Sloane walked down the boardwalk to the bonfire and watched the sun set fire to the sky, listening to the surf rush into shore as the sea breeze blew good vibrations their way. As usual, the children were running around the compound, laughing and yelling.

Cape Cod Hospital, Hyannis

Seth sighed. Recovery was hard, and he didn't like it one bit. *I sure don't feel like a bloody hero or savior, that's for sure. Well, the bloody part fits. Damned fish. Luckily, I didn't lose my foot, but I'll be missing that pound of flesh in my leg. I don't like the talk of physical therapy either. I have things to do . . . places to go. What about Janie? Monalisa has to recover, too. What about* Wing It *and Bradford Sail Inn? Wish I did have a coat of shining armor. My foot hurts. My damned leg hurts. Doc says I'll be in here for at least a week. Shit. I can't do shit lying here. I hate hospitals.*

Seth fumed at the nurse hovering over him. "No damn it, I do not want to blow into this stupid lung sucker thing for fifteen breaths."

"That is a spirometer. It's breathing exercises, Seth." The nurse remained cool and calm.

Seth did not. "It's a pain in the ass."

"At least your lungs don't hurt as well. Try again."

Seth swore at the nurse and grudgingly acceded to her request.

A short while later, he berated his physical therapist. "What kind of physical therapy is this? Old man exercises?"

Undeterred, the physical therapist repeated. "Ten leg lifts. One, again, two, again . . ."

Seth fumed as an orderly wheeled him back to his room, chomping at the bit and not a happy camper. His hands gripped the edge of the sheet that covered his damn leg. He was sore. And he was mad at his progress or lack thereof. He hated that he tired so easily, wanting more than 30-minute physical therapy sessions to hurry things along.

They wouldn't let him use his cellphone, and the landlines were useless. Hank had assured him that things were under control. Moreover, Seth heard that Sloane was taking on his tours. He tried to feel gratitude, but the truth was, it grated on him. *It's not enough that she swiped my plane, but now she's stealing the show. She's even made changes in how tours are booked. Okay, so doing business online is working, but my kiosk deserves more than a* Gone Fishin' *sign. Oh yes, I heard about that all right. And somehow, she talked Monalisa into similar upgrades with* Bradford Sail Inn *business. She has no business —*

His brain stopped his tirade.

Bradford Sail Inn *was* her business, too. She was a *partner. Well, her actions aren't exactly silent now, are they?*

To top things off, the doctors weren't so pleased with his progress either and threatened to keep him longer if he didn't settle down. *I'm about as down as I can get. I'm fuckin' depressed.*

When I'm not mad that is.

On the day of Seth's release from the hospital, he was still grumbling to anyone who would listen.

Then Sloane, wearing a mask, waltzed into his room and kissed him on the top of his head. "Here I am. Sloane to the rescue."

He growled. "Kissing through a mask. Wonderful. Thank you, Center for Disease Control, nobody believes you anymore."

Sloane kept her tone upbeat despite his scowl. "What's the matter?"

"That's some hello. Are you going to pat me on the head, tell me I'm a good boy, and then pet me behind my ears?"

Sloane quirked her brow. "Not a good enough welcome? Need some petting do ya? Just behind your ears? That's all?"

Still grumbling, Seth barked, "Hardly."

Sloane walked to the door, apparently checking to be sure the coast was clear of any medical personnel. Then she sashayed over to him, lifted her mask, tilted his head, and kissed him long and slow while petting his head. "Good boy," she crooned. She ran her fingers through his hair and finished it off by blowing in his ear. "Satisfied?"

He grimaced. "Not quite. You probably gave me COVID." He was still crabby, even after all Sloane had done for him—helping Monalisa, looking out for Janie, keeping his businesses going, visiting him, and now kissing him.

She fanned herself, looking aghast and innocent. "Moi? What?"

He grumbled, "You took my plane."

Sloane shot back. "I left you a note."

"I got your note."

"You're just mad because I stole a page from your playbook—or in this case, flight manifest. At least I wasn't joyriding. I had to see my attorney fast."

Still unmoved, he groused. "You need one for the charges I'm pressing. You're stealing my business, too."

"We're partners, *partner*. I'm earning my keep. You gotta practice what you preach, buddy. I'm *helping* you run the business."

He still felt out of sorts, not used to having help.

Sloane frowned at him. "Are you mad or depressed?"

"Both. I don't need help."

"Said the spider to the fly. We've had this conversation already."

"Maybe. But now I've wised up. I understand how you felt when I tried to help you."

Sloane strode over to his bedside and leaned over. "Look, maybe you were too nice to me when I was not accepting your help, but I'm not you, and I have something to say, mister."

"What?"

"Get over yourself."

Chapter Thirteen: Open Arms

Three weeks later, Seth still grumbled over his predicament. *Oh joy, I am the proud owner of crutches and a wheelchair. I should be thanking my lucky stars not acting like a dickwad, but there you have it.*

Monalisa had beat him home by a week or more. While she had to take it easy, wear a mask, and begin homecare physical therapy, he couldn't do squat. Literally . . . *I can't even manage a decent squat in physical therapy. Thank God, I can sit on the can.*

He was a little jealous that Monalisa could do some real work. She'd managed to cover the business end of both the Inn and her gallery since Sloane had updated things. Working on a laptop and supervising the kids with Addie's help was going quite well. Sloane sure seemed happy, too, enjoying the tours she booked on his behalf. *But I'm not happy. I feel guilty about feeling so shitty.*

One afternoon, Seth spotted Sloane's sketchbook sitting on the kitchen table. *Is looking at a sketchbook the same as reading someone's personal diary? An invasion of privacy? Nope, I hope. Besides, it's out in the open. In my house. Not as bad as stealing a plane.*

He knew Monalisa planned to commission several sketches for her Ole Paint Gallery. In pain but bored, he flipped through the pages. Despite himself, he chuckled when he came upon a series of Whaley drawings.

Whaley dragging towels from beachgoers, tugging on Janie's bathing suit like the old *Coppertone* ad, catching a flying frisbee, shaking water from his coat, doing a doggie sand angel, and one particularly poignant sketch of Janie burying her face in his fur while huddled into his big shaggy body.

Flipping through more pages, he saw seascapes of Race Point and the crashing sea, and another showed the paint mobile. That cheered him up somewhat, but he was just so flippin' mad at his slow progress and constant pain that he could scream.

No way in hell am I gonna go on pain meds, not after how booze got me in trouble. Bee balm, lavender, and peppermint might ease things, but they haven't cut the pain. Not even an axe can cut this shit.

Seth was grousing to Monalisa when Sloane sailed into the cottage, returning from a Circle Island Tour. She automatically kept him abreast of all things Wing It and Sail Inn — another of her innovations, claiming adding her name to make it Wentworth and Bradford Sail Inn sounded terrible. Sail Inn did have a nice marketable ring to it, he admitted with a grudge. *Pushy broad.*

Sloane's upbeat chatter usually calmed him, but low clouds were moving in, and his attitude worsened with the coming storm. It was promising to be a doozy.

Sloane frowned at him. "You're as gloomy as the weather promises to be. Reports say we're in for a nor'easter. Is that usual this time of year? I'm just glad there are no other flights scheduled for today."

Monalisa cocked her head. "This time of year, a nor'easter is uncommon, but having said that, we got a tornado in Harwich in twenty-nineteen, and no one expected that. Usually, we don't get tornadoes. Maybe three or four in the history of Cape Cod. Nor'easters are more common in winter, late fall, sometimes March . . ."

Seth's morass expression probably gave away his mood, but he chimed in anyway. "Nothing's been usual since

COVID, if you ask me."

Monalisa wagged her index finger in his face. "Stop it. This isn't like you. What's your deal? Feelin' sorry for yourself, are you? Cuz you're hurting? Everyone here is, too. You're the captain, so buck up or shut up. You're an old seadog. Act like it. Don't set a bad example for the young scallywags."

"They're fine," he grumbled.

Sloane looked around. "They're awfully quiet."

Monalisa spoke up when he just shrugged. "They're looking for sea glass. Probably down the drift line beachcombing with Addie."

Sloane must have noticed her sketchpad in his lap because she pointed at it. "Make yourself useful. Select three sketches you think Monalisa might like."

"Why can't she choose her own?"

Monalisa yawned and snapped her answer. "Because I'm taking a nap — doctor's orders — and she asked *you*, Joe."

Sloane made puppy dog eyes at him. "Humor me."

Seth hmphed and started flipping through the pages. Sloane seemed happy to watch him looking carefully at each drawing.

"These are good, Sloane, they suck you right in." Then he winked. "And you draw people in with your work."

"Lame," was all Sloane said, but humor sparkled in her gaze.

He looked at the sketches again. "I can feel the wind and taste the salt in the air of this one. It even looks salty like I can taste it." He tilted the sketch toward her so she could see.

"I call that one *Adrift*. It's how I felt when I got here, so alone. I like it, too."

He went back to flipping pages and paused on one that took his breath away. It was one of him and Janie, her feeling for him evident in the lines Sloane had used to render the look and light in Janie's eyes. He cleared his throat several times and fought off tears before asking, "What do you call this one?"

"*Devotion.*"

He set the pad aside and swiped his knuckles across his eyes. "I'm an asshole."

"Sometimes." Sloane pushed another set of pictures into his hands. "I need one more."

He took them without saying a word and noticed the subject was *him*. When he was coming out from the ocean looking . . . well, damn good. He glanced at other drawings of him when he was pensive, like a few minutes ago, or vulnerable with Janie huddled into Whaley. Looking invincible and proud landing a striped bass. Wet with water glistening and running off his shoulders. He wondered how she managed to catch his spirit when he was flying or how intent he appeared bent over the drift line, looking for sea glass.

Seth browsed picture after picture of himself in every mood and action. The one he held in his hands now showed him smiling with love in his eyes.

Sloane had depicted a sturdy guy who took action. A man who threw his head back, laughing at danger but not afraid to be gentle. A man who looked whole—foot or no foot, limp or no limp—alive and well. She had captured him in every mode and manner she could.

He looked at her. "What are these?"

Her answer was slow, and she appeared thoughtful. Finally, she looked him straight in the eye. "You. How I see you. What I see when I look at you. That is the man I see."

He flashed her a half-smile. "Where's my pirate hat and peg leg?"

She bopped him in the head with a couch pillow.

"What do you call these?"

Her tone was even but soft, breathless. "*The Sea Savior Series.*"

"Seriously?"

"Yup."

"Are there some of you? Self-portrait or something? Any drawings of us? Seems like you've been saving me and my . . . bacon."

"*Our* bacon."

Seth smiled and winked. "Yeah, that's what I said. Our business. Saviors, rescuers, heroes. It looks good on you, Sloane, and makes you *my* shero."

"Right back atcha, Captain." She saluted.

"Is it just me, or is life giving us a mulligan?" he murmured.

She raised her brow. "A do-over, eh?"

"Somethin' like that, yeah."

Sloane looked thoughtful. "Well, Whitt did say love isn't algebra. I remember him saying something like, *It's simple addition. One plus one.*"

"Plus, one I'd add," he said.

"How so?"

"You, me, and Joel."

She winked. "Makes three. Add one more . . ."

"Janie . . . and it's four." He chuckled. "We're pathetic."

Sloane laughed. "Looks like we're launching a new chapter, charting a new course, filing a new flight plan." She looked at him. "Care to add any metaphors I missed?"

He grinned. "I think you got all the bases covered."

Sloane pushed Seth's wheelchair out the door onto the boardwalk overlooking the shore and loosened more than the pirate scarf binding her hair. She had kept her promise to Whitt and could finally let her troubles, worries, cares, and concerns blow away in the sea breeze. The Tradewinds carried them away, taking her fears, too, replacing them with new dreams and promises.

The healing ocean winds of Cape Cod offered her another merger between sky and sea . . . between her and Seth. In the contrails, she chartered her path to a future with a new version of happily ever after.

She clearly saw the path to navigate, hopefully avoiding its updrafts and turbulence. She throttled up, realigning her sights. She knew she had rescued Seth and his business and accepted that he had saved her just long enough to see how to save herself.

"Are we on the same flight plan now?" she whispered, bending to kiss his lips. "Promise me that we're on the right flight this time."

He returned the kiss and nodded. "I promise."

Needing neither a figurative wing nor a prayer, united, they flew into their sea breeze future, fully expecting a happy landing.

The End

More from Kathy

The Beach Series

Beyond the Beach Book One
Beyond the Beach Book Two
Beyond the Beach Book Three
Beyond the Beach Book Four
Beyond the Beach Book Five
Back to the Beach Book One
Back to the Beach Book Two
Promises on the Beach

The Mountain Series

Mountain Hot
Mountain Christmas
Mountain Skye Prequel to the Weather Girls
Mountain Kiss
Mountain Joy
Mountain Promises
Mountain Holly
Mountain Silver
Mountain Mistletoe
Mountain Bred
Mountain Led
Mountain Wed
Mountain Hookup
Mountain Fever

Mountain Due
Mountain Bachelor
Mountain Match (coming soon.)

Cape Cod Series
Cape Cod Promise Book 1
Cape Cod Connection Book 2
Cape Cod Christmas Book 3 (coming soon)

ABOUT THE AUTHOR

Kathy Kalmar, born in Detroit, Michigan, lives with Larry, her husband of four decades. Lately, she feels her life has recovered from the bad country song-like life because her Smoky Mountain Tops Round House is rebuilt from the 2016 Chimney Tops II Wildfire in which she is writing her next book in her Writing Room. Her current residence is enlarged by four feet with the addition of their new puppy. She loves to read and write contemporary romance novels. Meanwhile, she remains fond of hot tubbing, chocolate, and sipping wine and mai tais and moonshine whether at home, Waikiki, Cape Cod, or Tennessee. Y'all come back, hear?

Contact Kathy at KathyKalmar.com

www.ingramcontent.com/pod-product-compliance
Lightning Source LLC
Chambersburg PA
CBHW060644130626
46555CB00002B/946